No Rest for Slocum

locum felt like he'd only slept ten minutes when Rosa woke im. "Three men are coming."

"Good." He stood up and checked his Colt out of habit. He lled the cylinder on his sleeve, looking at it in the dim light ith care. Satisfied, he closed the gate and reset the empty nder the hammer.

"Hold up!" Jim shouted and used a rifle shot to punctuate is order. In the confusion, the riders' horses bumped into each ther and unseated one rider. Cussing filled the night.

"Get off those horses." Slocum was there. He caught the owned man by his collar and stood him on his feet with the x-gun in his right fist.

"You sonsabitches—" His words were cut short when Slo- ım busted him over the shoulder with his gun butt and he rumpled to his knees, screaming in pain.

Slocum gave the man's butt a boot and sent him sprawling n his face in the dust. "Shut your mouth and stay there."

The third man threw his hands up higher, and O'Riley jerked is six-gun out of its holster. Jim held the rifle muzzle on them.

"Where is the stolen race mare?" Slocum demanded.

The one on his feet shook his head. "How should I know?"

"Someone better know or I'm going to notch your ears until hear the answer." Slocum holstered his six-gun. Then the blade f his large jackknife glinted in the starlight after he opened . "Who's first?"

JAKE LOGAN

SLOCUM AND THE DIAMOND CITY AFFAIR

JOVE BOOKS, NEW YORK

THE BERKLEY PUBLISHING GROUP
Published by the Penguin Group
Penguin Group (USA) Inc.
375 Hudson Street, New York, New York 10014, USA
Penguin Group (Canada), 90 Eglinton Avenue East, Suite 700, Toronto, Ontario M4P 2Y3, Canada
(a division of Pearson Penguin Canada Inc.) • Penguin Books Ltd., 80 Strand, London WC2R 0RL,
England • Penguin Group Ireland, 25 St. Stephen's Green, Dublin 2, Ireland (a division of Penguin
Books Ltd.) • Penguin Group (Australia), 250 Camberwell Road, Camberwell, Victoria 3124, Australia
(a division of Pearson Australia Group Pty. Ltd.) • Penguin Books India Pvt. Ltd., 11 Community
Centre, Panchsheel Park, New Delhi—110 017, India • Penguin Group (NZ), 67 Apollo Drive,
Rosedale, Auckland 0632, New Zealand (a division of Pearson New Zealand Ltd.) • Penguin Books
(South Africa) (Pty.) Ltd., 24 Sturdee Avenue, Rosebank, Johannesburg 2196, South Africa

Penguin Books Ltd., Registered Offices: 80 Strand, London WC2R 0RL, England

This is a work of fiction. Names, characters, places, and incidents either are the product of the
author's imagination or are used fictitiously, and any resemblance to actual persons, living or dead,
business establishments, events, or locales is entirely coincidental.

SLOCUM AND THE DIAMOND CITY AFFAIR

A Jove Book / published by arrangement with the author

PUBLISHING HISTORY
Jove edition / November 2012

Copyright © 2012 by Penguin Group (USA) Inc.
Cover illustration by Sergio Giovine.

ISBN: 978-0-515-15119-0

JOVE®
Jove Books are published by The Berkley Publishing Group,
a division of Penguin Group (USA) Inc.,
375 Hudson Street, New York, New York 10014.
JOVE® is a registered trademark of Penguin Group (USA) Inc.
The "J" design is a trademark of Penguin Group (USA) Inc.

PRINTED IN THE UNITED STATES OF AMERICA

10 9 8 7 6 5 4 3 2 1

ALWAYS LEARNING   PEARSON

1

Slocum rode down to Diamond City, Arizona, from Silver City, New Mexico, on a stout, Roman-nosed bay. Dressed like an ordinary drifting cowboy, he felt ready for a bath and shave when he rode into the crossroads town in the moon lake country that straddled the New Mexico–Arizona Territory border. To the southwest rose the purple heights of the Chiricahua Mountains like the body of some sleeping Apache giant.

Diamond City contained no such precious stones. It was just covered in the light brown dust driven by stiff hot winds that swept up from Mexico. The hovels of adobe included a cantina, a small store, what could barely be called a hotel— some shabby furnished rooms with narrow cots—and a livery made up of a few crooked stick corrals that sat beside it. Three sun-bleached wooden water tank wagons were parked close by. Painted on the side of them was Water For Sale—5 Cents a Gallon.

Slocum dropped out of the saddle, and his ugly headed bay horse put his muzzle down, snorting in the dust like he'd punctuated the end of their journey. He wrapped the reins on the worn-smooth hitch rail. Out of habit, he reset his gun belt, took off his hat, and wiped his gritty face on his sleeve. His face was burned from the sun's reflective rays. He wondered if there

1

was any escaping the blazing heat of the ovenlike winds. The batwing doors of the cantina creaked when he parted them.

The room's stale interior was dark after the brilliant midday sunshine. He let his eyes adjust to the dimmer light. A Mexican bartender nodded to him. The man had a black mustache and brown eyes that bored into this stranger in deep inspection.

"Good afternoon," the barkeep said in Spanish.

"Yeah," Slocum said to the man. "Send me over a glass and some whiskey." He noticed some card players on his left who showed some mild interest in his entrance. They represented no threat as far as he could see. With a toss of his head toward a side table where he could drink with his back to the wall, he headed there. His run-over boots and spurs clunked across the hard dirt floor as he moved to his chosen site.

A slender Mexican girl delivered his liquor. Slocum thought she looked neither real pretty nor very smart. She set the unopened brown bottle of whiskey and a tumbler on the table and stuck her white palm out for payment. "Four pesos."

"He wants all of his money now?" Slocum asked without a grin, stretching his leg out to draw some money out of his pants pocket.

She glanced back at the bartender and asked him in Spanish. "You want it all now?"

The bartender, with no hesitation, told her, *"Sí."*

Slocum slapped four silver cartwheels on the table. Then he stopped her and, between his fingers, held up another coin of the same value.

She frowned at him.

"This one is for you. For later on."

A grin filled her full, dark lips at the glimpse of his money and his intentions for her. "That will be fine. *Muchas gracias,* señor."

He kept the coin from her. "What's your name?"

"Rosa."

He rose up, leaned over, and kissed her on the forehead. "Rosa, now you go find me a good supper and bring it to me. I'll pay you for that too."

"Oh, *sí,* señor."

He gave her the coin, which she dropped into her small cleavage, then she scooted the coins for the bottle of whiskey off the table into her hand.

"Your food will be coming—" She winked at him, seeming excited about their future date. "Me too, later."

"Yes." With a chuckle, he raised the brim of his hat and then straddled the chair to sit down again. He reached for the large folding knife sheathed on his gun belt and opened the razor-sharp blade to cut the tax stamp and seal holding the cork on the bottle. After returning his knife to its sheath, he used his teeth to wrestle out the cork, then poured two fingers in the glass, set the bottle down, and tossed back the first draw. The fiery liquid cut a path across his dust-clad tongue and down his throat, warming its way to his belly. It also loosened some of the slimy phlegm behind his tongue, and he cleared it to spit aside on the floor.

A short white man in a green-checked suit came over from the card game. "You a cowboy?"

"What do you need?"

"I—I don't need just a cowboy. I'm a businessman. But someone stole some valuable horses of mine."

"Apaches?" He frowned at this man's mumbling. He must be drunk.

"No. I think they were cowboys that stole them."

"Are you asking me to go find them? Why?"

"'Cause you look tough enough to get them back. I'd pay you fifty dollars to get my horses back."

That wasn't enough; he didn't work that cheap. "What kinda horses were they?"

"One is a Kentucky Thoroughbred stallion. The other, a racing mare bred to him."

"What's your name?"

"Casey O'Riley. What's yours?"

Slocum poured himself some more whiskey, then looked at the man's red freckled face. "Have a seat. They call me Slo-cum."

O'Riley's green eyes stared at him hard. "Will you look for them?"

"How long have they been gone?"

"Two, three days."

"What's the law doing about them?"

"Nothing." In defeat, O'Riley slumped down in the chair beside Slocum and thumped his face down on the tabletop. "I'm going crazy. I have to find them. They're all I've got left."

"You want a drink?"

"Whiskey won't solve my problems. I've tried that already." He swept his wild reddish hair back from his face and shook his head, sitting upright in the chair once more. "I lost my wife, I lost everything. . . ."

"Aw, hell, it can't be that bad. Did you trail the thieves here?"

"I tried. I took the stage from Tucson after I found they came this direction. Yesterday I learned they headed this way from Benson. But no one's seen them here. I don't know, I'm going crazy, I tell you. Those horses are all I have left."

Slocum sipped on the whiskey. So some men stole this man's Kentucky horses. "What happened to your wife?"

"She ran off on me with Cable Marky." He shook his head like he was lost. "I don't know where she went either."

"You better start way back there and tell me the whole story. How did you get to Tucson anyway? You aren't a native of that place."

"A man named Ira Moulton in Nogales, Sonora, wanted to buy those two horses. I told him I would need a down payment to get them there. I was in Kentucky at the time. I hired Cable and his brother Nichol to be my grooms and take care of the horses for me. They were professional track trainers and handlers. We came by train to the end of the tracks over there at Deming. My wife and I drove a buggy from there. Those two brothers rode horses and led those two of mine. I knew Cable was trying his damnedest to screw my wife—I told him I'd kill him if he tried to take her away from me.

"Ha, I didn't even have a gun. He knew it and he stole my wife and buggy and drove off from Tucson one night."

"Where did his brother go?"

O'Riley shook his head helplessly. "I never saw him again either. The next day I went to check on my horses and they said at the stable that the man I sent to pick them up had already taken them. And he gave me the letter that had my name on the bottom. It wasn't my signature, and from the description, the guy who took them wasn't the other brother. I never told anyone to steal my own horses. The sheriff in Tucson said if I could find the thief he'd arrest him. Arrest him, hell, I can't find my own ass out here in this godforsaken desert."

"Last place you heard the rustler had ridden through was over at Benson?"

O'Riley nodded. "Yes. Benson. They were seen there."

"But they aren't around here?"

"No."

"Tomorrow—can you ride a horse?"

O'Riley nodded.

"Good. Go rent one or buy one and we'll go look for them. They didn't go up in smoke."

"How—how much will you cost?"

"Five hundred dollars. When we get the horses to Nogales."

"Oh, good." O'Riley looked relieved and nodded thanks.

"You be at the livery at six in the morning ready to ride. Get a bedroll. We may be out in the cactus looking for them for days."

"I'll be there."

"Good, now go buy some clothes for the ride. Include a big straw hat or you'll be burned to a damn crisp out there in that damn sun."

As the man walked away, Slocum poured himself another half glass of whiskey. Rosa was coming. She set a tray filled with luscious-smelling food before him. The sweet aroma of cooked peppers, onions, and beef strips filled his nose. A stack of snowy flour tortillas and a bowl of refried beans sat beside them.

With a big smile, Slocum reached out and clapped her hand. "That looks damn good, girl. What do I owe you?"

"Twenty-five cents."

He paid her, and she leaned over and kissed him on the cheek. "I will be ready for you tonight, big man."

He sent her a sly wink and began loading a tortilla with

meat, adding some of the sliced hot peppers to the mix. Saliva flowed in his mouth at the first bite. Best thing that had happened to him since spanking a cute whore named Quin, and for that she had given him a wild night's fling in her bed up in Silver City's best brothel a week before.

The rolled-up tortilla filled with the spicy fresh ingredients settled him down. He forgot all about the blinding sun, the acrid dust that burned his eyes, and the deadhead ride from up in the mountains to these playas. His meal at last completed, he rose, corked the whiskey bottle, and started for the exit to go put up his horse.

Before he reached the door, Rosa tugged on his sleeve. "Where will you be at, señor?"

"Isn't there a scrubby hotel here?"

She nodded.

"I will be there in a room when you get off work. Slocum's my name."

"*Sí*, Slocum." She stood on her toes and kissed him on the cheek.

He put Spook in the livery, paid the unbathed swamper, and went to the hotel. He rented a room from a grizzly old man who'd neglected to shave for a week. When Slocum paid him the fifty cents for the room, the man licked his lips, then tested both coins with a hard bite.

"Can't be too sure," he said in a rusty voice.

"Sure. There's a girl coming who'll be looking for me named Rosa. Send her to my room."

"What's her name?" The clerk licked the lead pencil and was poised to write it down.

"Rosa."

"R?"

"Yes, Rosa."

"R-o-o-s-a?"

"That'll do. Which room?"

"Number three."

"Number three, fine. You got any bathwater?"

"Out back, there is a tub." He tossed his unkempt, greasy gray hair toward the back of his head.

"Send me some hot water."

"Cost you two bits."

"Gawdamnit, get the hot water." Fed up with the man's stupidity, Slocum slammed the quarters on the counter.

The man shrank away. "Yes, yes."

The people here in Diamond City were some of the dumbest in the world. Slocum went down the hall to the roofless bathing facilities at the back of the hotel. The adobe wall gave some privacy in a head-high pen that stank of soap and mold. He turned over the tub half-full of scummy water, which ran off and quickly soaked into the hard-packed ground. When the tub was back upright, he saw an older fat Mexican woman coming with two pails of steaming water.

"Gracias," he said to her as she poured the water in the tub.

Then two teenage girls brought two pails apiece. Neither one was pretty and they both looked fearfully at him, though he had never seen them before.

"We will bring six more," the older woman said and protectively herded the younger ones out of the enclosure.

He about laughed at her actions. "I won't bite them."

"It is not your teeth I worry about, señor," she said and left him.

They were back shortly. They dumped the hot water in the tub and set two full pails down for his rinse. He paid the older woman a dime. Then she bowed and said, *"Gracias,"* and left with her entourage.

When they were gone, Slocum undressed and hung his gun and holster on a straight-backed chair within his reach. He used a bar of soap he brought from his bedroll. When he'd finished soaping up, he rose and poured the first pail of water over the top of his head to rinse, then he finished with the last one. That would have to do for the moment. He got out of the tub and dried off using some stiff sack towels that hung on racks nearby. Then he put on his pants and carried the rest of his clothes and his gun to room number three.

In the room, he removed his britches and put his boots under the chair on which he piled his shirt, vest, and pants, then buckled his gun belt on the post beside the bed. He lay on his back and tried to imagine that after sundown his room might cool off some. Then he questioned where his good sense had gone when he'd offered to help the Irishman recover his horses. No telling how that would work—he doubted the man could ever take a long, hard-fought trail and capture the rustlers, but Slocum might be wrong.

Then a knock came on the thin door.

"Rosa?"

"*Sí*, señor."

"Come on in my oven."

She laughed and slipped inside. "I knew you were a big tease, señor."

When the door was closed, she flipped her shoulder-length black hair aside and put her back to the door. "You want to undress me?"

He sat up cross-legged on the bed and shook his head. There was enough of the bloody sunset's red light flooding the room for him to watch her undress. "I want to see you do it."

"Fine." She took the blouse off over her head. Her small pointed breasts shook when she threw the garment on the chair, then returned to her post.

"They are small, but they are sweet as honey," she said, cupping her breasts in her small hands and examining her pointed brown nipples. "In case you need some dessert."

Then, acting excited, she untied the dark brown skirt at her waist and stepped out of it, exposing her glass-stem-shaped legs and the black patch of pubic hair. The skirt joined the blouse in a short toss. "Now you can see all of me. I am not as pretty as some girls, but I am also not as fussy as some of them either."

She wrinkled her nose at him, seeming a little uncomfortable standing naked in the glaring red light pouring into the hot room. "Do you want me?"

"Of course." He nodded. "Come over here."

She obeyed and climbed atop the bed on her knees, inching toward him until he reached out and pulled her to his chest. Then he kissed her hard on the mouth and her eyes blinked in disbelief, but her arms quickly encircled his neck and she returned his effort with a hot tongue.

"Oh, señor." She nearly swooned. "You didn't come to simply fuck me. You came to make love. Yee-ha! Oh, hombre, you are going to be fun—" Her small hand sought his dick and she began to pump his limp tool awake. He lifted her up and tasted her nipples, which turned out to be as hard as a rock, and she pushed them at him. They did taste like honey and she was fast turning into a hot fire. The idea of having sex was fast consuming her brain and she twisted like a powerful serpent in his arms. He laid her on her back, then reached down and parted her stiff pubic hair with his finger and traced the damp slit, rubbing easily over the small clit and entering the lips of her vagina with his middle finger.

His actions made her gulp for air. "Oh, *madre de Dios*, that feels so good, I may go crazy. I would lock you in the calaboose—so no other woman could fuck you. Oh, my, you are driving me mad." She hunched her ass and thrust herself at his finger in a new fury.

His two fingers worked in easy to probe and spread her open. Her jacking him off was raising a great erection. Her breathing came in gasps, but she still fought harder and harder for him.

"Oh, señor, please take me!"

"I will. Keep going, you aren't quite wild enough—not like you will be soon."

His mouth and tongue fell upon her lips. She began shaking as he moved to mount her and she raised her knees to give him room to get into her. He realized how small she was when he lowered himself on top of her. In haste, she reached for his thick hard dick and stuck it in her cunt, then raised her butt off the bed so she could get as much of him as possible inside her squeezing pussy. Hard muscle contractions pulsed in the walls of her vagina and almost crushed his erection as he drove it in her again and again.

Ropes under the worn mattress creaked beneath them as he plunged in and out of her vagina. He wondered how rotten the ropes were and if they would break under all this activity. Rosa's bare heels beat a tattoo on the back of his legs as she seemed to cling to him for her life, her short fingernails gouging into his back like a bobcat attacking him.

She began moaning and he could see she was close to fainting. The dark pupils of her eyes were large, and she was clearly past seeing as her hair spilled around her face, veiling the features of her sharp nose and too-full lips. In the room's dimming light, she looked beautiful. The jiggle of her firm small breasts underneath him as he drove his dick into her harder and harder excited him more. His cock was soon jammed against the base of her works. He could feel the bottom of her womanhood and the flowerlike opening of her uterus when he came. Grasping both sides of her small ass, one half in each hand, he drove as deep as he could go and then the head of his erection exploded into a geyser.

She threw her arms out, swallowed hard, then fainted. A smile crossed his whisker-bristled mouth as he bridged her body with his dick still in her. Coming to after a moment, she half rose and searched around. Gently-like he began to poke her again and a smile split her mouth. Quickly she kissed his hairy chest and lay back down for more pleasure.

"You aren't finished with me, are you?" She shuffled her body a little bit underneath him. "I had a lover once who swore he would someday make me come. He never did, but I think"— she shrugged—"tonight you made me come, I know it now. I am a little sloppy down there. You want me to clean up for you?"

"No, I have lots more for you."

She threw her head back, laughed, and shook all over. With her fingers, she parted the hair at her forehead and pushed it in place beside her face. "I hope my heart is strong enough, hombre. You are a macho stallion."

After the third time they coupled, she collapsed and he curled around her warm, small body. Some women could surprise a man. Some never were aroused to having fierce sex, while others were like kerosene and burst into flames at the slightest spark. After a few minutes of lying on her side with her back to him, Rosa reinserted his still-stiff prick into her cunt from behind and then patted his leg. "Good night and *gracias*—I loved it so much, hombre. . . ."

2

The first rooster began crowing even before the dawn light awoke Slocum. By then Slocum and Rosa were no longer attached, and he slipped out of the bed slow and quiet so as not to wake her. He needed to find a vendor and get some breakfast. O'Riley would be waiting for him at the stable. There were stolen horses to recover, if they could find them. He dressed and strapped on his gun. He left Rosa two more dollars on top of her skirt and nodded good-bye to the sleeping form curled in a fetal position on the bed. *You are hell of a puta, Rosa. Maybe we will meet again.*

He set the weather-beaten hat on his head and eased out of the room. The clerk was snoring in a stuffed chair in the lobby. Slocum never woke him. He had not put on his spurs yet. Once outside the hotel, Slocum leaned on the wall and finished dressing. Spurs on his boot heels, he drew the six-gun and checked the five loaded cylinders before he pushed his shoulder off the adobe wall and went to look for something to eat.

He found an old toothless hag who squatted on the ground tending a small stove.

"What's for breakfast?" he asked her.

"A big tortilla, two eggs, goat cheese, some peppers, and well-cooked brown beans."

"*Bueno.* I will take one. How much?"

"Ten centavos."

"Cook it for me while I go get my horse."

"You must be in a helluva hurry, hombre." Squatted down, she crept over to get some things cooking on the small stove.

"Some men stole a couple of fancy horses. Have you seen them?"

"No. I never saw them. And if they'd come by, I would have."

"*Bueno,* then they're west of here." He left her and went for his horse, recalling how he had placed the half bottle of whiskey in his saddlebags. A good snort of that might clear the thick drainage down the back of his throat.

The sky was pink coming up over the New Mexico horizon. The cool air around him would not last long. He saw a hipshot saddled horse and a man under a great sombrero sleeping seated on the ground. That must be his man, O'Riley. He probably had been there all night, so as not to miss Slocum.

"Get up, hombre, and go get some breakfast from the old woman who's in front of the cantina. She's cooking mine and I will be up there in a short while with my horse."

"What's her name?" the sleepy Irishman asked, struggling to get up.

"Damned if I know," Slocum said and shouldered his saddle and pads to go catch his bay out in the pen. "She's the only one I saw."

"All right." O'Riley went stumbling off in the dust to find the old woman.

In a few minutes, Slocum joined him and paid the woman, who put the tortilla-wrapped meal in his hand. It was hot to the touch, and she almost had his partner's food ready.

"How far is it back there to Benson?" O'Riley asked him. "Oh, and I could have paid for this."

"Next meal, you pay. I got both of these. And Benson is, oh, maybe thirty, forty miles."

"You think you know where my horses are at?" O'Riley took a bite of his tortilla and went to fanning his open mouth. "Too hot."

"Hell, it was cooked on fire, what did you expect?" Slocum laughed at him.

His man yawned big. "I didn't get much sleep last night. I didn't want to miss you."

"Check your cinch and we'll head out. We can ride and eat too."

Slocum handed his wrap to the old lady and quickly checked the girth on his own horse, then mounted and retrieved his meal. Around a mouthful of food, O'Riley said, "I'm ready."

They booted their horses westward on the Tucson road. Someday there would be a railroad headed west on this tract, when the big banks let the money loose to build more miles. Financial markets reflected by the stock exchanges had the railroad stuck back at Deming for this year.

O'Riley kicked his horse up beside the bay. "What have you been doing that brought you to Diamond City?"

Slocum thought about telling him he'd been busy fucking a fiery woman in one of the finer establishments in Silver City, but that wasn't necessary. "Looked at some mines for sale, but none looked that rich."

"If I bought a gold mine, it wouldn't have enough gold in it to fill one tooth."

"You can be taken if you don't watch 'em. What did you do before those rustlers stole your horses?"

"I imported racing horses from England and Ireland and made some good money. I had one die coming over once and they buried him at sea. He cost me four hundred pounds and they gave me half his fare back. But after that, I only shipped them in the fall or spring."

"You have some more horses?"

"Yes, in the Adirondacks. I have six racehorses up there at the track and a man to train them."

"This stallion was a good one?"

"A wonderful horse. Never lost but one race. Finished second that time and they shouldered him hard coming out of the starting gate."

"Sounds like a good enough horse to steal."

"The mare was from the King George breeding line."

"I don't know about racehorse pedigrees."

"Well, these two certainly have an impressive ancestry. King George horses are hotly sought after in the racing circles."

"What can these rustlers do with them? Any lawman who knows horses will know they aren't simple ranch horses and ask questions."

"I have no idea."

O'Riley frowned at a burro honking behind them. Slocum turned in the saddle and saw the straw sombrero and the rider with a stick in her hand making the burro short lope. They had company. The hard-flailing rider was Rosa. A slow smile settled on Slocum's mouth. This business with O'Riley might not be so bad with her along.

Rosa reined her mount up and the mule, with the bit in his teeth, tried not to stop, but he was not dealing with a novice. The girl knew how to jerk him down.

"You going this way?" Slocum asked, amused and not at all unhappy to see her.

She nodded and looked upset. "You rode off without me."

"Did I say anything about you joining me?"

She shook her head. "No, but I'll be helpful to you."

He took his hat off and wiped his sweaty forehead on his sleeve. "There's a thought. Maybe you can be helpful. Whose burro?"

"Don't you know? Down here burros don't belong to anyone. You use them and turn them loose when you are done with them. The saddle and bridle cost me two dollars."

He gave a head toss at his man. "O'Riley, this is Rosa."

"I met him yesterday at the cantina," she said, not sounding too impressed.

The man nodded and reined his horse around to face her. "Good day, miss."

"Come on, you two," Slocum said. "We need to make it to Benson by dark today."

Benson was the last place he knew about the horses passing through. Their trail began there. Along with him, he had one lethargic guy he'd have to push to get to move and one honey-tasting titty girl. That should be a powerful enough posse to turn over an outhouse or two, and they were looking for some expensive racehorses stolen in Tucson. Plus, one of O'Riley's grooms had run off with his wife. She must be a dandy. No telling what else lay ahead for them or what he'd run across with this circus act looking for horse rustlers.

"Come on. We have to trot these animals," Slocum said and jabbed the bay in the sides with his spurs.

At Fort Bowie, no one had seen the racing horses. Not a mention either among the enlisted military men when he asked around if anyone had seen them. Horse soldiers would have been curious. Most knew good horses on sight. So they headed for the Dos Cabezas, the next stage stop up in the hills that gave it the name. There they found several dirty-faced miners sitting on the cantina porch drinking beer.

Slocum asked them about seeing two fancy horses. The rattle of their heads told him the animals had not been brought through there. He made the other two in his party water their own mounts again as they had done at the fort, and then they headed for Benson.

The next spot on the stage road was Dragoon Springs.

The stage station man standing on the porch met them. "Can I help you?"

"This man lost two great horses. A mare and stallion. Racehorses. You seen them come through here?"

The man shook his head.

Slocum dropped from the saddle to water his horse at the public trough. That was not good news. The thieves must have gone south from Benson. Slocum's belly was hollow from not eating since before dawn.

"Rosa, go find us some food." He tossed her a silver dollar.

"No, no." O'Riley made her give the money back to Slocum. Then he bought their supper—or gave her the money for it, anyway—and she went skipping off like a free spirit.

While the horses and her burro slurped up the water from the wooden trough, O'Riley asked Slocum about her.

"A nice young woman from back there," Slocum said, with a head toss over his shoulder toward Diamond City, where they'd met the night before.

"What does she charge?"

"A dollar, I guess."

O'Riley shook his head at the price. "I can get all the pussy I want for fifty cents."

Slocum shook his head at the man's attitude. "From your wife for free, if you ever find her again."

"That no-good bastard," O'Riley grumbled and scowled at the thought of the wife-stealing horse trainer.

Rosa soon returned with her two hands full of tamales, and they sat on the stage office porch, unwrapped the corn shucks, and ate them.

"What's next?" O'Riley asked. "My asshole is sore. I could sleep for a week. And still no horses."

Slocum looked at him hard in disgust. "Did I tell you this would be easy?"

"No, but—"

"That's right. Now stop your bellyaching."

They rode on through boulder-strewn Texas Canyon to Benson, arriving in the night, and ate supper in a small café they found still open.

"When she gets through eating, I'm sending Rosa up to the block of crib houses and see if they've seen your fancy horses. The rustlers had to go by those narrow cribs to have gone south to Tombstone. And those women don't miss much."

"Who are the ones that you want?" she asked between bites.

"They would have been leading two fancy horses, a mare and a big stallion. You don't have a good description of them, do you, O'Riley?"

"They are both fine, bay-colored horses. Heads high and powerful. The stallion has a scar, but you wouldn't see it unless you were up close."

"Oh, sure, if they went by, one of those *putas* would have seen them." Rosa jumped to her feet. "I won't be gone long."

"What help will she be?" O'Riley asked, disgusted, when she was started away from them.

"She probably can find out more from those women in half an hour than you or I could in a day or more."

"She's a whore, ain't she?"

"I don't know. She ain't run off with another man yet."

"Why do you keep reminding me about my damn wife? That money-grubbing bitch left me."

"Maybe because you treated her so nice is why she left you. You know, you are about the dopiest guy I ever met. You gripe even when folks are trying to help you for free and are doing their best."

"Hell, you'll get paid."

"Start paying me and her every day then."

"I need a drink."

"Sure, go blab off in some cantina and warn them bastards who've got your horses that we're coming after them. That's why I sent her. She can learn more from those sisters than you or I could spending a week in those saloons. Besides, the women won't mention she's been there."

"All right, all right. What do I need to do then?"

"Stop bitching. We will run these thieves down and get your horses back somehow. Be more helpful and damn sure stop treating Rosa like she's a slave. She came on her own and she can go on her own, anytime she wants. I figure she doesn't like working in a whorehouse, and she can be invaluable to us in this job."

"I never really thought about that."

"So now go back and tell me about your wife and the guy she left with. Did they take the horses?"

"No. I don't think so."

"Why not?"

"They left Tucson, and I learned that they went north. I think those two went to Preskit in my buggy. They have horse races up there, the marshal told me. Do they?"

"Yes, they do."

"They have races up there. He wanted to find another sucker like me and race his horses for him. No, I don't think they stole my racehorses. They just took my buggy and those two buggy horses. She could always say they were hers."

"Where did you meet her at?"

"At Albany, New York. Her father had some racehorses. I met her at the racing meet. She was a lovely young woman, though I doubted she was a virgin at the time. She got a little tipsy at a party one night and I seduced her, bent over at the waist in a cupboard closet in the kitchen. Very easily done, I might say. Later she told me she was concerned that her monthly event had not come—she said she was pregnant.

"I decided to marry her. Her father offered me a nice dowry. I accepted it and we had a bloody honeymoon. I doubt she ever was pregnant at all, but we took off from there to Maryland and raced at Baltimore. And so on, I watched her more careful so she didn't entertain any other men. I mean, she liked it rather well and it was very easy to, what do you say, to make her hot."

"Did she ever complain?"

"Oh, from time to time, she said, 'I thought you were more aggressive when I married you.' I guess that meant she needed to be bedded more often than I had time for."

"I see," Slocum said, still wondering if she and the horse groom she went off with had any part in the horse theft.

"Where will we sleep?"

"When Rosa gets back we can find us a place down on the river and roll out our bedrolls. I'm going to take a bath."

O'Riley looked dismayed at him. "Bathe in a small river?"

"It's free and I'll feel better when I get done."

They went out and sat on a small log bench to wait for Rosa's return. At least O'Riley didn't complain any more that evening. In an hour or so, she returned.

"I talked to a woman," Rosa said, "who thinks that Ike Clanton or his brother Billy met some man who brought the horses to Benson and he did business here with them. She said it seemed like it was set up in advance—like Ike knew the man would be bringing the horses."

"After that did she think Ike or one of their gang took those two horses to Mexico?"

"What does that mean?" the sleepy O'Riley asked, pushing his unruly hair back from his face with his palm and sounding half asleep.

"It means some tough gang of border outlaws stole your horses." Slocum hugged Rosa and kissed her. "You did great, darling."

"Yeah, yeah," O'Riley said. "I'm so damn tired I could sleep out in that damn street."

"Mount up. We're going to find a camp."

"Hell, I'll fall out of the saddle, I'm so sleepy."

"Come on," Slocum insisted, about to lose his temper at the dummy again. They had more problems than being sleepy if Ike Clanton had those horses. The Clantons had a damn fortress across the border where the gang hung out. Slocum had dealt with Ike, and the old man as well, a couple of times before. They weren't ordinary outlaws. They were established ones who used the border, and Old Man Clanton had all the government contracts to sell beef to the army and the Indian reservations—and most of that beef had been stolen in Mexico. The people below the border feared these outlaws as much as the widespread ranchers on the Arizona side did.

Someone had named them the Cowboys—with a capital C. When the Clantons weren't raiding ranches, they were robbing stages. Several of the Clanton gang, the old man included, had death warrants for several thousand dollars on their heads from the banking firms to be paid upon their deaths. They were the certain rulers of the border country.

"Who is Ike Clanton?" O'Riley asked as they approached the swishing sound of the river in the night. The San Pedro was never a big nor a deep river, but it ran good from the big springs upstream. Below Benson, a colony of Mormon settlers had irrigated quite a bit of land around St. David using the river and some artesian wells.

Slocum and his crew found a place to camp along the river, watered the horses and Rosa's burro, and hobbled them. They all had some jerky and feasted on the hard, dry, smoky-tasting meat, then Slocum took Rosa and his bedroll fifty yards upstream. He kicked branches and rocks away from a patch of sandy soil with the sides of his boots, then she unloaded the bedroll and straightened it out.

"I never asked if you were mad that I followed you," she said, undressing in the starlight.

"Did you think I was mad?"

"I hoped not, but I had fun with you last night and I said to myself, 'Rosa, he needs you for something.' " Slocum swept her up and closed his mouth over hers. Before his lips met hers, he saw the flicker of mischievous mirth in her dark eyes.

Her hard, small breasts felt good against his bare chest and her mouth opened as she surrendered to him. They were soon on top of the bedroll and his erection was poking her leg as he ran his finger around the rim of her cunt, and she raised her butt for his dick's attention. Her breath started coming in short gasps when he climbed on top of her and his hard-on slipped inside and through her muscled ring. As he began to pound her ass, her contractions added to the pleasure that lay between her silky legs.

Ah, Rosa was exactly what he needed. Exactly—and he was savoring his efforts to extract as much pleasure as he could possibly receive from her. He felt as heady as a soaring eagle as he moved over her, and each pistonlike plunge only renewed his desire for more and more of her body. Her heels beat a tattoo on the backs of his legs as they kept going and going. Then, when those two hot needles shot into the cheek muscles of his ass, he knew he needed to bury his dick in her up to the hilt and he exploded inside her vagina.

She fainted and he rose off her to curl around her from behind, throw his arm over her, and cup her right breast. He quickly fell asleep, and it was morning before the call of nature got him up and he went to the bushes at the edge of the small beach to empty his bladder.

Cool morning air swept his bare skin, and some topknot quail whit-wooed off in the chaparral. The relief of venting himself was a good one, and as he turned back, he heard Rosa rattle a coffeepot. She had started a small fire of dry sticks and squatted naked as Eve in the pink cast of light coming up over the Chiricahuas.

"What will we do today?" she asked.

"Go to Tombstone and see if we can find the racehorses or where Clanton's bunch took them."

"Will they be there?"

Slocum shook his head. He had no idea. Then he went to fill the coffeepot from the river. When he came back, she scolded him. "I could do that."

"You better get dressed. Screwball will be awake soon, and I don't want him gazing at your fine backside with hot desire."

She chuckled and rose to kiss him. Then she swept up her skirt and put it on. Her breasts fluttered when she wiggled into the blouse and concealed them.

"Is that better?"

"No, but better on account of him." He laughed.

She gave him a small push and chuckled at his words.

Breakfast was coffee and soda crackers. Slocum could tell that O'Riley did not like the menu, but it was all they had. It was still a good ride to Tombstone, but they could eat something more substantial when they got there later on in the day.

At about three in the afternoon they arrived in the sprawling mining camp on the mesa and dismounted at the hitch rail before a hole-in-the-wall café. The man who waited on them was dressed like a miner with hair covering his arms and more trying to crawl out from under his unbuttoned shirt collar. "What can I get you three?"

"What's on the menu?" Slocum asked.

"Thirty cents buys the daily special: beef stew and sourdough biscuits plus coffee. All you can eat."

The threesome nodded their heads, and the man shouted to someone in back, "Three stew orders," then went for their coffee.

The food's aroma was compellingly good and the first bite of stew filled Slocum's mouth with saliva. Much better than soda crackers. He finally picked up his coffee cup when he was halfway through the first bowl of stew and savored the brew. Not bad.

This midafternoon, the café had no other customers, and the waiter-owner struck up a conversation. "You all new in Tombstone?"

They allowed as they were.

"Well, we ain't had a knifing, killing, or dog shooting in five days and counting."

"Sounds peaceful enough."

"Wait till tonight. You'll think this is the Fourth of July. Well, Marshal White may keep it down, but when these Cowboys, as they call themselves, come to town, all hell will break loose."

"Thanks for the information," Slocum said. "We're looking for a couple of stolen horses."

"That can get you killed too, if the gang's got them."

O'Riley started to say something and Slocum cut him off. No need to advertise that they were there.

The man lowered his voice. "If I can help, let me know. I hate them bastards. My name's Cox, Hamby Cox."

Slocum gave him a head toss for him to come closer. "You ain't seen a fancy stud horse and brood mare come though here in the last few days?"

The man shook his head. "But you come back. Next time maybe I can tell you who has them horses. I've got some good contacts."

With a nod of approval, Slocum said, "We'll make it worth your time."

O'Riley nodded and looked as serious as he ever had since Slocum had met him back in Diamond City. He also paid for their meals, and they went out, mounted their horses, and rode out of town, heading for a ranch owned by a man Slocum knew.

Jim Davis had a place between Tombstone and Fort Huachuca. When they reached the ranch gate, Slocum dismounted and opened it. He'd called it a Texas gate: juniper sticks and a wire loop on the main post and a pry handle to put it back. Mounted again, he led off, following two wagon tracks through the stirrup-high dry grass.

"What's this friend of yours do?" O'Riley asked, looking over the flat country toward the Huachuca Mountains.

"Runs some cattle. He's a good man."

They passed a windmill churning up and spilling water out of a rusty pipe into a large homemade rock-and-mortar tank. Some topknot quail scurried across the wagon tracks and went into the bunch of grass on the opposite side of the road.

An adobe jacal sat under a few small cottonwood trees beside some pole corrals. A bowlegged man came out on the palm-frond-shaded porch and rolled himself a quirley. When he lighted it, the wind soon swept away the smoke and he studied them, finally nodding with recognition.

He tipped his well-worn felt hat at Rosa. "By God, where've you been, Slocum?"

"Over in hell checking on my friends. Jim, this is Casey O'Riley and that's Rosa."

"Well, by God, girl, you're riding with a tough bunch, ain't you?" Davis said to her.

His words brought a small smile to her mouth, and she aimed it at him. "No, they are good hombres, señor."

"You can call me Jim."

She agreed and jumped off her burro. "How can I help you, Señor Jim?"

"Come inside my casa," he said, offering her his arm. "We'll make them hombres some fresh coffee. You two put them ponies in the corral. Where do you hail from, Rosa?"

She laughed at the big flirt. "A small village in Sonora."

"I've been down there many times. What village?"

"Los Nigra."

"Why, I've been there too. I bet I knew your momma." Laughing, the two disappeared inside the jacal.

"Is this a safe place?" O'Riley asked, looking around the greasewood-clad prairie like he might find trouble there.

"Yes, much better than Tombstone. Those Cowboys have ears that are too big. Clanton pays for information about threats to him or his operations."

O'Riley nodded and began to undo the girth on his saddle. "How will we ever get out of here if we do find my horses?"

"Leave that to me. I worry more about finding them than how to get them out."

"I ain't bitching. I appreciate all you've done. But if they got such a communication system, how do you think we can rescue them and get away?"

"I promise you. We get them and we'll get away. Once we get them to your buyer, they're his problem." Slocum lifted his saddle and the wet pads off his bay horse. "We need to buy Rosa a horse. Riding that damn burro would wear out a saint."

"How much will one cost?"

"Thirty dollars."

"I can buy it."

"Take it out of my reward."

O'Riley laughed, shaking his head in surrender. "You don't have a single doubt in the damn world that we're going to find them."

"That's right." Slocum shut the gate on the bay. He never had any doubts until something was over. Nothing took the strength from a person like a defeatist attitude.

"What's next?"

"After dark, I'm returning to Tombstone. I have some friends there who might help us learn more. A drunk Cowboy may talk. Liquor loosens tongues. And they can sure drink when they get cut loose."

"You need me?"

"Not unless you want to go along."

O'Riley wearily shook his head. "I'm going to sleep a couple of days."

"Fine." Be the best thing he could do. Then Slocum wouldn't need to nursemaid him around.

Rosa came out with two coffee cups, one in each hand. She gave O'Riley one and Slocum the other. "It is hot," she warned them.

Slocum thanked her, and with his arm over her shoulder, he herded her to the squaw shade behind the jacal.

"Jim is a sweet man," she said privately to Slocum.

"A good one. I'm going to Tombstone after dark."

"What should I do for you?" she asked.

"Rest here. I'll be back before dawn unless I get a good lead. I'm going to try to buy you a horse to ride too."

Her face brightened at his words. "I don't want to be any burden to you."

With a shake of his head, he dismissed her concern. "You need one to keep up with us. Besides, I need you."

She blushed. "Good. I am having fun riding with you. Do I need to do more?"

He shook his head. "You're fine."

"Good. You be careful then."

"I will."

He wondered about the night ahead. Could he filter out some leads about where the horses might be? That would be his purpose—and to not expose too much of his hand to the Cowboys while he was at it. Ready to try, he closed his eyes and silently asked the powers that be for help.

3

Tombstone lay swallowed in darkness, save for where light from various establishments flowed out on the boardwalks and into the street. A screaming, wild whore was in some guy's arms and being packed out the swinging doors of Big Nose Kate's Saloon. The whore's stocking-clad legs were thrashing like a paddleboat and she was trying to slug her abductor with her fist.

The customer must have been drunk, because her efforts weren't stopping him. Slocum stepped up behind the man. "Put her down or I'm blowing daylight through you."

"Huh?" The man dropped the whore and she scrambled like a runaway chicken to get under the batwing doors. When she was safely inside, Slocum heard her say, "That crazy sumbitch was taking me away."

A man shouted, "He'd gawdamn sure have brought you back."

Raucous laughter came from the saloon.

"Where the hell's your gun?" the big galoot demanded, weaving on his boot heels on the saloon's porch.

"It's gonna be up your ass if you don't move aside."

The big man swung at Slocum. He missed and Slocum drove a fist into his gut, doubling him over in agony. Unable to get his breath and bent over, the man oohed and aahed, holding his arms up close to his body. With his boot, Slocum gave him a shove that caused him to sprawl on the boardwalk. Then, disgusted, Slocum went inside the saloon.

"Hey, bitch," someone shouted at at the whore, pointing to Slocum. "There's the guy that saved your ass."

She jumped up from some guy's lap. Hands on her hips, she stalked over to Slocum. "Well, what do I owe you for saving my ass, buster?"

"Nothing, darling." He turned to the bartender and ordered a double.

"Well, that settles that." She made a big show of going back to her former cohort, and laughter followed her.

"Your name ain't Slocum, is it?" the bartender asked in a low voice.

"Who's asking?"

He made a slight head toss to the right and lowered his voice further. "The guy on the end of the bar. Frank Holt. He's with Wells Fargo."

Slocum caught the man's eyes and nodded. Then, turning to gaze into the mirror behind the bar, he studied the faces in the smoky haze over his shoulder. None looked familiar. Maybe Holt knew something about the two stolen racehorses.

The barkeep soon brought Slocum a note on a paper napkin.

Meet you out front in a few minutes. Holt.

Slocum pocketed the message and then paid the barkeep. He downed the last of the hard whiskey and left the barroom for the night outside. Holt came out and saw him, then turned and went into the alley.

A few minutes later, Slocum joined the shorter man in the alley, where they shook hands and exchanged greetings.

"I'm looking for two horses," said Slocum. "Thoroughbreds, mare and stud. Ike Clanton picked them up in Benson a couple of days ago. They were stolen in Tucson."

"I've not heard about them. But if I do, I'll let you know by general delivery."

"What are you working on now?"

"A robbery, of course. We shipped several thousand dollars to Nogales from the local bank here. There was a driver and two shotgun-armed guards. They and the money have gone up in smoke. They left here at daybreak four days ago and no sign of them or the rig or team has been seen since."

"Clanton's bunch behind it?"

"I figure so. I get some information from an informant over there from time to time, but nothing has come out from there about this one."

Slocum nodded. "I hear anything, I'll contact you."

"I'd appreciate that. How come you're turning down pussy?" Jim chuckled.

"Too much mouth and ass on her for me. She'd probably talk my dick off."

"You're probably right. Thanks."

Slocum dropped in on two more of the more prominent saloons, then he rode back to the ranch under the stars. Except for Holt's troubles with the stolen money, he knew little more now than he had to start with.

Back at the ranch, Slocum found Rosa in the bedroll, and when he pulled off his boots and clothes to join her, she woke up.

She propped herself up with her elbows behind her. "You find out anything?" she asked, sounding sleepy.

"No, nothing on the horses, but Clanton's bunch must have robbed a buckboard hauling money to a bank in Nogales four days ago, then hid the rig, guards, and driver. They've just vanished."

"That's a lot to go up in smoke." She held up her arms for him to come down on top of her.

When he discovered that she was naked as a jaybird under the covers, he almost laughed. She was ready for his return, sleepy or not. He kissed her and they locked mouths, and it wasn't long before he was stiff enough for her to put him inside of her and squirm around to get comfortable. Oh well, there were lots worse deals than Rosa. And he savored their love-making as their pace grew faster and faster with both of them headed for a high peak, finally ending in an explosion inside her tight vagina.

"Oh my," she said, sounding weary. "That was wonderful." Then she rolled over and went right back to sleep. Slocum didn't find it that easy getting shut-eye when thoughts kept kicking about in his mind, like where did they'd take O'Riley's horses? And where had the disappeared rig with all that money gone? Wondering about the fate of the driver and guard was something else to make him roll over on his other side and try again to sleep.

At sunup, Rosa and Jim fixed breakfast. The rancher was having lots of fun cooking with her. They were laughing and teasing each other the whole time. But Jim wasn't hard to like. Slocum had known him for several years and considered him one of his best friends.

O'Riley joined them, still half asleep, while they were putting the platters of scrambled eggs, fried bacon, fried German potatoes, and sourdough biscuits with white gravy in a big bowl on the table.

"Is it Christmas?" O'Riley asked, looking it over. They laughed.

Slocum told O'Riley what he'd learned about the horses—nothing—then about the robbery and disappearance of the entire outfit.

"Where in the hell could they hide a stagecoach?" Jim asked as they devoured the breakfast.

"It may have been a buckboard, but that's what Wells Fargo wants to know," Slocum said.

"What do we do today?" O'Riley asked.

"I want to ride down into Mexico and talk to some people I know there."

"Can I go?" Rosa asked.

Slocum nodded. She might learn more than he could force out of some of them.

"Take my horse," O'Riley said to her. "I'm going to sleep. I haven't had enough rest yet."

With the tin coffee cup in his hands, Slocum considered

where they might go first. "You have any opinion on where we should go?" he asked Rosa.

"Los Nigra."

"I don't recall ever being there." He shook his head. "Will we need our bedroll?"

"We can take it along. It is a fair distance down there. You have never been there?" She looked a little taken aback when he confirmed that he hadn't. "Then I will show you that place."

With a swish of her skirt, she went to get their bedroll. Slocum looked to the underside of the wood shakes overhead for help, then smiled and told the other men that they'd be back whenever they could get back there.

Both men laughed.

"Bet he ain't in any hurry to return," O'Riley said, "not with her along."

Jim agreed and they all laughed about it again.

4

They didn't reach Los Nigra until late afternoon. The small village was a "high in the sky island." It was much like the Chiricahuas and Mount Grant, where in the high altitude, they found a different climate than the lower desert country, cooler and filled with pines. A spring-fed stream had silver trout that darted for cover at the first shadow of a man walking by. There were small plots of land along the creek that the people irrigated for fruit trees and grape vineyards. Alfalfa and vegetable gardens adjoined the creek, where they saw one small aqueduct that took water uphill to irrigate some higher land.

Slocum stopped at the cantina in the village. Rosa introduced him to Paulo, the bartender, who reached over the bar and kissed her on the cheek. "Good to see you, my darling," he said in Spanish.

"Good to be home, Paulo. We are looking for some stolen racehorses."

He shook his head. "I have not seen them, but they could be at Pico's. He handles some horse deals that are not always right, huh?"

She nodded. "*Sí*, I know about him."

"Who do they belong to?" the bartender asked.

31

"A man we work for." She indicated Slocum, who was beside her sipping on his double shot of mescal.

"You sure found yourself a big man, Rosa."

She laughed. "And no one bothers me."

"I bet not."

"Who's Pico?" Slocum asked her privately when her friend moved to get another man a beer.

"A small-time outlaw who lives north of here." She wrinkled her nose. "But I doubt he has such valuable racehorses."

"But he might know about them. These people have a wireless telegraph up here—sometimes they know before the rest of the world knows."

"Oh, yes. Can we stop and see my grandmother for a short while?"

"Sure."

She hugged his arm and proudly smiled up at him. "She will like you."

Leading the way, she found the short, little, fragile-looking lady working in a fancy, weedless garden. "Grandmama, this is my friend Slocum."

A warm smile crossed her wrinkled face. "Ah, he is a *mucho grande* hombre."

Her arms were raised high for him to hug her, and he swept off his hat and bent over to lightly squeeze and kiss her. Where his lips touched, her hand quickly caught the mark under her palm and her eyes twinkled. "You are an exciting man."

"You must have been exciting yourself when you were a girl."

She nodded, amused. "But there is no one left alive who can tell you if I was."

They laughed and went with her into the jacal. "You must have good help; this place is so neat."

"My great-grandchildren spoil me helping me keep this place so tidy. This is my granddaughter Nana, who lives with me. Nana, here is Rosa come to visit, and this big hombre is Slocum. Can we feed them?"

"Oh, *sí*, Grandmama. We can feed them. Come inside."

Slocum herded them inside the adobe house, put his hat on

a wall peg, and looked around at the paintings on the wall. He pulled Rosa aside. "Who did this art?"

"Grandmama did it, but look over there. She taught Nana how and she is surpassing Grandmama now."

"Does that upset your grandmother?"

"No, she wants Nana to become a master. That is her goal."

"How long can you stay?" Nana asked Rosa, who looked to Slocum for his answer.

"Only an hour or so," he said. They needed to go find this man Pico's place, the ranch that the bartender had mentioned.

"Then will you sit for me now?" Nana asked him.

"I guess."

"Rosa, come with me." Nana said, taking her by the hand toward the kitchen. "I'll explain the food you need to fix. I want to sketch him. Are you all right, Grandmama?"

From her woven rocker, the old lady smiled and nodded. "If my eyes were not so dim I'd want to catch him on canvas too."

Nana brought a tall, three-legged stool when she came back, and she seated Slocum on it. She pointed to a mark on the wall for him to look at. Then, using a sliver of sharpened charcoal, she began tracing in his face on a canvas. Her fingers worked fast as she looked up and then reproduced on canvas the lines that she observed.

"We're searching for some fancy racehorses that were stolen in Tucson over a week ago," he said, noticing the horse pictures on the wall.

"Who stole them?" Nana asked.

"We don't know. One of the Clantons' men picked them up in Benson and whisked them away."

"Ah, the Clantons." Nana lowered her voice. "Those devils are not worth spitting on. They came here six months ago, and some of them raped women and took anything of value."

"Did they bother you?"

She chewed on her lower lip, and Slocum saw tears flood her lashes until she turned away. "Yes. Three of them— kidnapped me."

He had his answer and it made him mad. A nice-looking girl near Rosa's age, who didn't deserve to be raped. The Cowboys were hard-hearted, but they needed their balls cut out for doing that to a young woman like her.

"You have some names of the ones who attacked you?"

"Gorman, Valdez, and Bach were the ones who kidnapped me."

"What do you remember, and what can you tell me about them?"

"Gorman has a scar above his right eye. A thick one. He's a short and fat gringo. There are scars on his belly from knife fights. He was shot sometime in the left shoulder—you can see the powder burns around that scar."

"How old?"

"Maybe thirty-five or forty. His hair is wavy and has some gray."

Slocum nodded. "Who else?"

"Valdez has blue eyes. He is mostly Mexican. He lost the bottom two fingers on his right hand. Short, he was maybe in his midtwenties."

"The third man?"

"Adolph Bach was German. He talked like one. Maybe five foot eight. Big black beard, steel gray eyes. A very ruthless, mean man." Her shoulders shuddered under her blouse, obviously from the bitter recall of her horrible experiences with the men.

"If I ever find them, I'll even the score for you."

She nodded without a word.

"I have the food ready," Rosa said.

"Feed Grandmama and then you can feed him where he sits." Nana laughed and took another hard stare at her subject before making more marks on the canvas. "I am coming along fine."

"Good. Slocum, your face may be as famous as the *Mona Lisa* in Paris after this," Rosa teased him.

"Or keep the ravens out of her garden in place of a scarecrow."

The girls snickered.

Rosa fed him the tortilla-wrapped beans and meat.

"That's good food," Slocum said, chewing on his bite, and winked at Rosa.

After Slocum finished his meal, Nana wound up her drawing and brought the canvas over to show her progress.

"Is that all right?" she asked, showing him the sketch.

"Sure, that's me." He winked at her. "Nice job."

"I'll get our horses," Rosa said.

"Yes, Grandmama, we are going to leave you." He strode over to stand in front of her.

"You are a nice man. I will burn some candles for your safety while you are looking for those horses."

He hugged her gently and patted her back. "Be good."

"Oh, I have to be, my big man."

They laughed and he kissed Nana on the cheek. "I will find your attackers."

She nodded silently.

Slocum and Rosa went on. She knew where the man Pico that the bartender mentioned was located. They rode across a narrow mountain pass and down the western slope. The place they found was snuggled in a valley.

"You want to stay up here while I ride down there and see him?"

She shook her head. "I am not afraid when I am with you."

"It could be dangerous if we find those horses up here."

"Let's go. I have been thinking ever since we left Grandmama and Nana. I did not know anything about Nana being raped." She looked sad riding beside him.

Slocum nodded. "Those Clanton men are brutal bastards."

She agreed.

He led the way and rode in through the front gate of the ranch. Some stock dogs began to bark down by the jacal. A woman in her thirties came outside and frowned at them. Hands on her ample hips, the buxom woman shouted something that Slocum couldn't hear. He watched for any threat she might call up.

"What's his name again?" Slocum asked Rosa as they approached the screaming woman.

"Pico. I don't know her." She shook her head with a serious

frown about what the woman in charge was doing down by the casa.

"I'm watching her," Slocum said under his breath.

"Is she calling for some gunmen?"

"I see some men coming from those buildings over there."

"What is your business here?" the dark-haired woman shouted. "This is a private ranch."

"Is Pico here?" Slocum asked. Obviously it was siesta time, and these sleepy-eyed farmhands were hardly pistoleros, but he didn't lower his guard.

"No, he is away on business."

"That's good. May I look at your horses? I am looking for some expensive racehorses stolen up in Arizona."

"No." She shook her head. "We have no damn stolen horses here."

"If they're here you better surrender them. The *federales* will treat you much tougher than I will. I simply want those two horses back."

"We don't have your damn horses!" she shouted at him and stomped her foot, then she wouldn't move aside and blocked his way.

"This damned ugly horse will run you over, woman. Now move," Slocum said to her.

At last she retreated and he rode by. He stood in the stirrups as she continued to chew him out verbally and traipsed behind their horses. No sign of a stallion in the horses he could see in the pens.

"Look in that shed," he told Rosa. "Ride over there."

She short loped her horse and halted him at the open door. "No horses in here."

"I told you we had no horses belonging to you."

"Why did you deny us a chance to look for them if you aren't hiding them?" Slocum asked.

"This is our ranch. You have no business being here. Don't ever come back either."

"Fine, we'll leave." He booted his horse, Rosa did the same, and they rode off the place.

"Don't you ever come back!" she shouted at their backs.

He'd be certain they didn't.

Slocum and Rosa returned to the village and stopped at her grandmother's place. No news. Slocum knew he had to learn whether the horses were at Old Man Clanton's ranch, but he couldn't do it himself. He figured he'd need an Apache to enter that compound and let him know about them or to ride them out, and he said as much to Rosa.

"Do you know any Chiricahuas we can hire to go look up there?"

"Maria's husband, Benny, is one."

"Good. Who is he?"

"We can go by their place on the way back to Jim's ranch," Rosa said, turning to glance back and then twisting forward in her saddle again. "Boy, I can't get over that bitch back there. Pico's new woman is a mess."

"Didn't you know her?"

Rosa shook her head and wrinkled her nose. "I never saw her before. He changes women quite often."

He reached over and clapped her on the shoulder. "She was all mouth and ass. No worries. Now let's find this Apache."

They rode up to Maria's place and scattered her bleating goats when they entered the yard. A woman in her thirties came from the squaw shade, drying her hands, then she recognized Rosa and openly smiled.

"This is Slocum," Rosa said as she dismounted and ran to hug her friend.

"Good day, señor," the woman said. She used her hand to shade the bright sun.

"He needs to hire your man," Rosa said.

"Oh, Benny will be here in a moment. He is cutting wood, but he will hear you are here. What kind of work does he have to do?"

"Spying."

Maria nodded. "He will like that."

Rosa agreed. "I thought so too."

Maria's husband appeared and for a moment stopped to size up Rosa and Slocum. Then he smiled at Rosa.

"Long time we no see you," he said to Rosa.

"I have been away working. Benny, this is Slocum. He needs some help."

"Sure, sure. It is good to see you again, Rosa. You look happy. He must be a good man."

"He is. He really is."

"Come in the shade," Maria said to Rosa. "I have some new material to make a dress."

"Oh, that sounds wonderful." They went under the thatched-roof squaw shade.

"What do you need me to do?" the man, who certainly looked Apache, asked as he squatted in his knee-high boots facing Slocum.

"Have you ever been to Old Man Clanton's ranch?"

"Yes, but that is a bad place to go for a man who likes to live."

"I am looking for two horses. A stallion and a mare that were stolen in Tucson and taken there, I think."

"What should I do about them if I find them?"

"Find them there, I'll pay a twenty-dollar gold piece. You bring them out, I can pay you fifty dollars."

Benny whistled through his teeth and held his right knee with both hands as they squatted. "That is *mucho dinero* for a poor man."

Slocum agreed. "My man can tell you what they look like."

He made a distrusting face. "I hate to scout at night. I know that is a fable of my people, but I worry about such things. Dying in the dark, you know?"

"I do know all about your fears." All Apaches feared being killed in darkness because they believed that if that happened, their spirits would never get out of this world to the other one.

"How soon must I go?"

"We are going back to Jim Davis's ranch tonight. Meet us there."

"I know Jim." He nodded that that was no problem. "I will be there in two days. I may find a friend to help me."

"Just so that the Clantons don't know what we're doing." Slocum listened for his reply.

"Ah, *sí*. This man won't tell them nothing."

"Good. Here is five dollars in case you need some things."

He paid the man in silver cartwheels that clunked into his hand. Both of them rose, then shook hands. Two days to wait wasn't long at this point. Those horses might be there and if so, Slocum could have O'Riley on his way to Nogales with them soon. The final page in his diary would be they were delivered. Slocum nodded to Rosa that he was ready to leave and thanked Maria for her help. They left for Jim's place.

They avoided any crossroads, stores, or settlements. Slocum didn't want attention drawn to their passing through. The Clantons paid for any and all information that might be had in regards to them. Not much moved or went by in the border country that they didn't know about.

It was late when they reached the ranch. On the way in, Rosa promised to cook him something, since it had been long hours since they last ate. A sleepy-eyed Jim got up from his bed and asked how things had gone. He also told Rosa there were beans cooked and she could reheat them. In minutes she had the wood cookstove heating and was making tortilla dough.

"I found an Apache to go scout inside the Clanton stronghold and see if the horses are in there. He and another will be here in two days, and O'Riley can tell him how to identify his horses."

"Sounds like you did some good." He went by and kissed Rosa on her proffered cheek as she worked on the dough. "You should find yourself a real man," he said to her.

"I will think about it," she promised, laughing and shaking her head at his teasing, busy making the food.

Slocum just about fell asleep in the chair at the table. If he'd been by himself, he'd have eaten some jerky and gone on to the bedroll—but he wasn't going to disappoint Rosa since she was making such efforts for him.

Jim talked about the mining business, but he said the main silver and gold was under the mesa that Tombstone sat upon. No one else had made another major strike.

"That's been the thought all the time. Ed Schieffelin had found the main easy one that came to the surface and that was it. Lots of folks had been led to it in the past by hired Mexican guides who, in the end, murdered them and took the high-grade stuff they'd dug up. It had been a good racket until Ed found the site."

"That's why he called it Tombstone," Slocum said. "Those soldiers over at Fort Huachuca told him all he'd find out there prospecting would be his own tombstone with all those Apaches running around in that country."

"Bet a bunch of them enlisted men wished they'd looked some for it. Hell, it wasn't fifteen miles from the fort where he found the vein." Jim shook his head. "Why, I probably rode past it a dozen times back then when it was just some Mexican's scratchings."

"No doubt, and Ed also sold out and has the money in his pocket." Slocum shook his head. He knew the man. Big mining took big bucks, and the treasure vein could have shifted under the earth and they'd never find the rest of the gold and silver.

Rosa handed Slocum some food wrapped in a flour tortilla. Slocum took a bite and smiled. "This is worth missing sleep over."

Rosa smiled and then yawned big. His words pleased her enough to draw a smile. When they got in the bedroll, they were both so dog tired they passed on any notion of sexual activity and fell asleep when their heads hit the bedding.

His plans now in place, Slocum would have another day or two to wait for the results—but those Apaches would soon know whether or not the Clantons had O'Riley's horses.

5

The next morning, Slocum had to explain his plan to O'Riley, who looked no more rested than he had before Slocum and Rosa went to Los Nigra, despite his long naps in their absence.

O'Riley's bleary eyes appeared glazed over. "So I am to describe the horses to them and they will go look for them. Right?"

"That's the plan. I promised them fifty dollars if they can get them out."

"Good idea. What if they can't get them out?"

"Then we go to my next plan: We go get them."

O'Riley's green eyes flew wide open and his jaw sagged. "Is—isn't that dangerous?"

"Hell, ever since we took their tracks it's been dangerous."

"I guess you're right. I won't deny that I am a coward. If I'd been more of a man, that damn horse trainer would never have dared take my wife."

Slocum agreed. "That's spilt milk. Think about the future. Getting those horses back. And maybe after that you'll have enough spine to go find her."

"You make it all sound so damn easy. I don't know." O'Riley shook his head in disbelief.

"Start thinking like a man. If you really want your wife

back, you go up and kick that horse trainer's ass and take her back."

"We'll see."

"No, we'll do it."

"Maybe with you along. Maybe I don't want her back, you ever think about that?"

Slocum shrugged. "We'll see when the time comes."

O'Riley left him and headed for the house, mumbling to himself.

"What's wrong with him?" Rosa asked, catching up with Slocum and brushing out her hair as she strode beside him.

"Oh, he's not sure he wants his wife back."

"So?"

"He needs a rod stuck up his ass to straighten his spine is all."

With her laughter ringing out, she clutched his arm, thoroughly amused. "I think you're serious."

"I am." Then they both laughed.

Later, Slocum rode into Tombstone by himself. He wanted all the information he could gather. In the Alhambra Saloon, he spoke with a man he knew from the Denver gold strike, Al Hudson. They took a back table with a bottle of whiskey and two glasses. The place was quiet.

"How's Tombstone?" Slocum asked, pouring some liquor in his friend's empty tumbler.

"Oh, like all boom and bust towns. The mines are keeping the whorehouses open."

"Subsidizing them?"

"Hell, yes. Them madams know how important they are and can get money out of the mines to keep them going and keep prices low enough the miners stay and fuck the whores instead of going home. Those workers make good money, but the mines don't want 'em to get a pocketful and go home. Gamblers are the same: They get money too from the mine owners to skin the working men so they remain broke and have to stay."

"How much do they get?" Slocum was interested in his theory.

"Madam Lou Ann took her business sheet for last month's take to their accountant and they paid her five hundred dollars to supplement her income. They say Big Nose Kate was paid seven hundred bucks." Hudson shook his head. "It would be better to have a whorehouse than a small mine, huh?"

"It might be. I've got a tougher job. I'm looking for a race-horse stallion and mare. You heard of any for sale?"

"No, but Ike Clanton said he had a new one that could out-run the damn wind. He was drunk as a hooter and telling any-one who'd listen he owned the fastest horse in the world."

Slocum scowled at the man's words. "He don't own him, his men stole him. When's he going to race him and where?"

"I think down on the border next Sunday."

Slocum frowned hard. "Won't bring him over into the Ari-zona Territory, will he?"

"Hell, no. I hate that big mouth sumbitch. How are you going to get them back?"

"I'm working on it." Slocum took a sip of his liquor.

"Well, lots of luck. Why don't you shove your six-gun up Ike's ass and blow the top of his head off?"

"Not a bad idea. They ever find the stage the Clantons robbed?"

"It was a buckboard." Hudson shook his head and moved his glass over for Slocum to refill it. "I bet it's in the Clanton compound."

Their conversation broken up by his deep cough, Hudson shoved himself up from the table and bent over as the seizure continued. At last he used a handkerchief to clean his mouth and nose. He gasped for air and said, "I been in them damn mines too long."

Slocum agreed, deciding Hudson had contracted TB. Shame, he liked the guy, but it looked like the disease was fast consum-ing him. He poured Hudson more whiskey—life on the frontier was tough as nails. One day you were robust, the next dying slowly from a vicious disease that rotted out a man's lungs.

He parted from Hudson and went to the hole-in-the-wall café. Cox, the owner, nodded. "You're still up and taking nourishment."

Slocum nodded and acknowledged him. When Cox was sat-isfied they were alone, he took a stool beside Slocum and asked him if he'd heard anything about the horses.

"Still looking."

"You probably need to talk to a whore that Ike's sweet on."

"Who's she?"

"This week, he's been—" He lowered his voice. "It's Handy Ranny."

Strange name even for a whore. "Where does she work?"

"Got a crib of her own south of that train depot that they're building. Anyone can point it out to you."

The young woman with straight, light brown hair who worked for Cox delivered Slocum's bowl of stew. He would have guessed she was sleep deprived, but he saw little in her thin form to indicate she was a sex bunny. But no one ever knew about females; some came in plain wrappings, but were wild and sexy in bed.

Cox brought him coffee. Almost protectively, Cox watched the young woman retreat toward the kitchen door before he turned back to talk to Slocum. "You got any other leads on the horses?"

"Not much." Slocum started on his food with a spoon. Salvia flowed in his mouth at the first taste. "You make good stew."

"Thanks. Where did the red-haired guy and the cute girl go?"

"They're resting."

"He have lots of money?"

"Most of his money is in those two horses."

The man nodded. "So he's broke."

"That's why we need his horses back."

"Good luck."

"No word on that buckboard that disappeared?"

"All's quiet. I guess the Clantons know where they buried it, and the men's bodies too."

Slocum stopped. "Buried it?"

"Hell, yes. It's the only way it could have disappeared. I bet they hired some Mexicans to bury it all. Them Cowboys are work brittle."

"That's a new idea." Slocum nodded and considered his next spoonful of stew, thinking about how he could find out about them.

He went to find Handy Ranny's place. He walked the distance and found her jacal. At the closed door, he rapped on the wooden panel.

"Yeah, who's there?" The raspy female voice sounded drunk.

He heard the door being unbolted and looked in at the pale face of a white woman, maybe in her midtwenties, whose blue eyes looked to be swirling. "Who *dee* hell are you, mister?"

"A friend. Let me in. We need to talk."

"You got a big dick—" She hung on the side of the half-open door.

He pushed his way inside. She staggered back and at last swept the dull blond unruly mop back from her face. Feet apart, unsteady-like, she put her hands on her hips, and the gown she wore gaped open and exposed her right breast and a large brown nipple. Slocum shut the door, not looking back, and stared hard at this loop-legged woman.

"I charge five dollars." She tried to straighten up, but soon slumped down her shoulders as if out of the energy to hold her stance. "I'm tired of standing. Let's get in bed."

She covered her nakedness by jerking the gauzy dress around to cover her exposed tit. "Come on."

Turning on her bare heels, she headed for a large, tall bed that took up most of the jacal. She stopped and lifted an open wine bottle, then drank from the top. Large bubbles went up inside the bottle. Setting it down, she turned and looked back at him. The back of her hand wiped part of the wine from her mouth. "Get your damn clothes off, you aren't bashful."

"Maybe I don't want you."

With her palm on the sheet, she slumped in defeat on the bed and shook her head without looking back at him. "Do I have to beg you?"

He stepped over close and hauled her up in his arms. "I came for information. Does Ike Clanton have a new stallion?"

"Stallion? Ike? No, he's got a small pecker. He ain't no stallion." She wiggled her hips and then pressed her breasts against him. Her efforts caused the filmy garment to fall off her into a pile at her feet. "Well, here I am."

"Think hard. Does Ike have a new stallion?"

"Maybe. Get in bed with me now and when you get through

with me, I'll tell you all you need to know." She motioned for him to come on and her voice turned to pleading with him. "I need you now."

"If you are lying to me I'll cut off all your hair."

With effort, she crawled on the bed, exposing her bare ass to him, then flopped down in the center. "Is that too much to ask?" she said.

He bolted the door. Then he went over as she drunkenly sang some song about a wild . . . horse. "Oh, wild horse, where are you—"

Raised up on her elbows, she looked lost in her dreams as Slocum began to undress. "I got feelings. I may be a whore, but—I got . . ."

Naked at last, Slocum climbed on the bed and crawled over to her. He parted her legs. She was too drunk to do much else to help. "Get your knees up."

Numb, she obeyed and he moved through them. His erection entered her and she swooned and hugged him. "Feels gawdamn good. . . ."

He gave her his hardest efforts until she fainted. He knew dealing with a drunk woman was never wonderful, but he finished on her limp form anyway. What had he learned? Nothing. Searching the small jacal, he found some water plus a towel and cleaned up, then dressed. She'd proved to be a waste of his time. The strong winey smell of her body embedded in his nose, he set his hat on his head and adjusted the gun belt on his waist. In disgust, he looked at her naked body sprawled on the sheets—he'd simply leave her for Ike and get out of there. He couldn't squeeze answers out of a woman rough-like without his conscience biting him.

The Apaches were his only lead now. But as superstitious as they were about doing things at night, they still might back out of the deal. Stopping in the street, Slocum looked back at the whore's closed door and shook his head in disgust. What a big waste of his time.

He realized that two men were following him, being obvious by turning away whenever he stopped to check who was behind him, walking up the boardwalk, heading for the Oriental Saloon. He ducked into an alley, his hand resting on his gun butt. By law he was supposed to have already checked that pistol in at the nearest establishment when he entered town. But the opportunity had not availed itself for him to do so. He felt grateful to still be wearing his gun and holster.

Two men raced to the gap opening of the alley. They stopped. "Where in the hell did he go?"

Slocum, pistol in hand, stood between two buildings and could see them clearly. When they'd run by him, he stepped out behind them and ordered them to halt. They wilted in their tracks.

"Who are you?" He checked them from behind for weapons with his left hand. He found none.

"What?"

"Spit out your names and who you work for while I consider how I'm going to kill you two."

"What do you mean?" the shorter one snarled.

Slocum slammed him on top of the shoulder with his pistol barrel. The man screamed in pain and fell to his knees.

"Now talk." His patience thin, Slocum was ready to do more damage to them.

"Bob Taylor," the shorter one said.

"Gunner Blythe."

"Who do you work for?"

"Old Man Clanton."

"Why are you following me?" When they didn't answer him, he kicked the one called Blythe in the butt, who went down onto his knees next to Taylor.

"We're just following orders," Taylor said.

"Tell the old man to mind his own damn business. And I'll put a damn bullet in each of your heads if you trail me again. You savvy me?"

"Yeah."

"Then get up and run for your horses." Slocum stepped back, realizing he'd warned the old man and the whole clan that there would be trouble between him and them.

He watched the two run for the far end of the alley. They weren't Clanton's toughest men. But they might ride on too.

They'd looked scared enough when Slocum finished with them. Maybe his Apaches would find those horses—if they showed up.

He went back to the ranch and Rosa ran out to greet and hug him.

"How did it go?" She was excited by his return.

"Where do they race horses across the border?"

"Maybe at Engles?"

"Good. You know the way there?"

"Sure. Will his horses be there?" she asked.

"They say Ike is bringing a fast horse. It could be O'Riley's stallion."

"What horse?" the sleepy-looking O'Riley asked, combing his too-long red hair with his fingers.

"Ike, maybe, racing your stallion over in Sonora on Sunday."

"Really? What can we do?"

"Probably not much except watch. He'll have plenty of his men there to be certain we can't claim him."

O'Riley's shoulders slumped. "What good is that?"

Slocum shook his head. "If we can find out where he's at, then we can try to get him back. Right now we don't know jack about the horses' location. The law in Mexico won't help us either. He has them bought off."

"This gets tougher sounding to me."

"Did you think they'd simply give them back?" At times Slocum couldn't believe this man's attitude toward their situation. Sometimes he wished he'd never gone to Diamond City and met O'Riley. But then he wouldn't have met Rosa either.

"Hell, they don't steal horses where I came from."

"Welcome to the Wild West of the Arizona Territory then."

"You hungry?" Rosa asked Slocum.

He nodded. Mostly he wondered if the Apaches would be there later. Things were sure heating up. He wanted this deal over, maybe then he'd take Rosa down in the Madres and cool off some when this horse recovery was over. That girl was a damn sight more interesting than most of the men around him. A damn sight more.

6

Apaches never simply rode up. They came like smoke, and their path was many times unknown. Benny came to the ranch in the twilight on the second day. Slocum knew there was another figure with him in the shadows of the night.

The three spoke quietly in the growing dark away from the ranch house, around a campfire. "This is Iron Hand," Benny said, and the man squatted across from Slocum nodded.

After Slocum told Benny and Iron Hand he thought the horses were at the ranch, he went inside the house and brought back O'Riley, who was awake for the first time in days.

The Irishman described the horses' coloring to the Apaches, then told them the most distinctive feature: the stallion had a scar on the left side of his neck, obvious enough. Those two animals no doubt would be separated from the other horses. If the chance came to steal them, the stallion was the one to recover.

"Be careful. Tell me what you find," Slocum said to the Apaches.

The two agreed and were gone like the smoke from a campfire. Slocum and O'Riley went back to the house.

"Did they come?" Rosa asked when he came inside.

Slocum nodded.

"What did they say?"

"They're going to try to find the stallion. If they can get him out unharmed, they will."

"When will we know? You didn't ask them when they'd be back," O'Riley said.

"When they find out. Apaches do not come like family and bust down your door. They come quietly so no one knows when or why."

"Hmm. That's strange."

"No, that's an Apache. Ike's been bragging when he gets drunk in Tombstone that he is going to race a fast horse next Sunday down in Sonora. So if the horses aren't at the old man's place, Ike has them someplace else. That's what I figure."

"Can the Apaches find that place?" Rosa asked.

"I have no idea. But, Rosa, you and I are going down Sunday to watch. Two men were trailing me in Tombstone the other day. They work for the old man. So he knows I'm looking for the horses."

"How did he do that?"

"Hell, he pays for any information that might be useful to him."

"What can we do about it?" O'Riley looked impatient.

"Wait and see."

He nodded at Slocum that he understood. "That ain't easy when your whole life's savings are tied up in a couple of damn horses. What will I do if I don't get them back?"

"Find a real job."

O'Riley shook his head. "I have no skills."

"You get hungry enough, you'll find them." Slocum could recall once cleaning out a livery barn that was so deep in horse-shit and stinking old hay that a man couldn't stand up in it without bumping his head on the beams. Cleaned out, he couldn't touch the loft rafters short of standing on a ladder. That job didn't take skills, only a manure fork to pitch it on a wagon and then pitch it off. O'Riley could do that all right.

Rosa had supper ready and she called them to the table. Jim Davis was flirting with their cook when they came into the room.

"By God, this gal never fails us," Davis said, amused about something. "Slocum, you're damn lucky to have her."

"I'm damn lucky, Jim. What did you do all day?" Slocum asked him.

"Oh, shooed some of my cows back in the direction of the ranch. They were heading for the Mule Mountains, and it's hard to get them out of the junipers up there."

"I would have gone along and helped you," O'Riley said.

"Thanks, but I can handle it myself. Maybe you'll get your horses back."

"I sure hope so."

They ate supper and Rosa did the dishes. Slocum dried them. O'Riley and Jim played checkers. Then Slocum and Rosa excused themselves and headed for their bedroll beyond the corral. After a quick roll in the hay, they went to sleep.

It was before dawn when Slocum woke up and discovered an Apache squatted beside him.

"Benny?" he whispered.

"*Sí*, señor."

"Was the horse there?" He swept the covers back and sat up in the starlight.

"No."

"Thanks."

"I spoke to a man I know. He said that the stallion *had* been there and Ike had taken him away. He works there and will not tell anyone else. He said the mare had never been there."

"No idea where she might be?" He put his hand out to silence Rosa after discovering she had woken up.

Benny continued, "He said only the stallion was there for some time. No mare."

"Ike's been bragging that he has a fast racehorse. Where is he keeping him?"

Benny shook his head.

Slocum paid him ten dollars and thanked him. Benny nodded and said something in Spanish that Slocum couldn't understand, and the Apache left them.

"What now?" Rosa asked.

"We go to the races Sunday."

"What if he has the horse there?" She quickly dressed.

"We'll see what we can do to get the horse away from Ike."

"Won't he have men there to protect him?"

Slocum shook his head, seated on his butt and pulling on his boots. "Probably, but you never know about Ike."

Once he was on his feet, he hugged her and they went to the ranch house together. Their arrival and lighting a lamp awoke the other two men.

O'Riley shielded his eyes from the light. "Any news?"

"The stallion is not at the old man's place now, but he was earlier. Ike moved him. I'm not certain when. The mare was never there. We think Ike took the stallion someplace south of the border and he intends to race that horse on Sunday."

O'Riley nodded. "Is that the next place we go?"

"Yes."

"You think this Ike has him now?" O'Riley asked.

"Best I can tell. I'm going to Gleason to buy Rosa a horse today." What he really had in mind was seeing if Ike was over there. He spent lots of time drinking at Gleason because he hated the Earps so much. The Earps ran Tombstone, and anyone else in power either owed the Clantons favors or, like Sheriff Behan, was in the Clantons' pocket. The Earps arrested some of their men and were not making life easier for the Clantons and their underhanded operations.

Slocum knew Wyatt was suspected of murdering four gang members who had held up a stage between St. David and Tombstone. Wyatt tracked them to the Whetstone Mountains, where the robbers were jumped in camp by him, a Wells Fargo Agent, and a scout named Mickey Free who found them. These men supposedly gave them a fight, lost, and were shot and buried. Word was out that they had been executed, shot in the back of the head. But no coroner court was held about the men's demise. No one said who shot which one. They weren't the first criminals who met Wells Fargo's idea of justice. Just talking about robbing a stage or holding up a bank was enough to sign your own death warrant. One night four unemployed ranch hands were overheard talking about pulling a stage robbery. They rode out of town and were never heard of again.

Slocum knew even more stories about the power of the Clantons. The express agents no doubt were looking hard for the buckboard that had disappeared on its way to Nogales.

Come daylight, Slocum rode for Gleason on his Roman-nosed horse. Midmorning he reached the town, which was sleepier than Tombstone, and went into the local saloon. At the bar, he ordered a beer and could not see Ike among the loafers. Some famous gunman from Texas sat at a dimly lit poker game. Slocum knew him well enough to nod to, then he turned back to ask the barkeep about a horse trader.

The thin man in the soiled apron gave him directions to Herman Roach's place. Roach was supposed to have some saddle horses for sale. Slocum paid for his beer with a dime and left the sour-smelling saloon. Grateful to be outdoors, he rode up the creek and soon found a steam-driven sawmill and ranch. Under a cowboy hat and wearing overalls, a big man headed down the hill when he caught sight of Slocum as the large blade whined through some sweet-smelling saw logs.

"My name's Roach. What can I do for you?" the big man asked, offering his large paw to shake Slocum's hand.

"I need a saddle horse for a lady."

"I've got a nice bay gelding. Five years old, he's been rode a lot on a ranch, but he's sound. Might do."

"How much is he?"

"Twenty-five."

"A saddle?"

"I don't have any new ones, but I got a good used one for twenty bucks. It's sound and it'll do."

The gelding was easily caught and acted all right when Slocum checked him out in the corral. He led him out and then tossed the worn saddle blankets on, followed by the well-used saddle. Rosa would be proud of the deal, and he paid Roach the forty-five dollars. They shook hands and the big man shoved his hat back.

"What brings you to this country?"

"I'm looking for a Thoroughbred stud and mare that were stolen in Tucson and brought over here."

"Who stole him?"

"I'm not sure, but I think Ike Clanton has him now."

Roach's eyes narrowed. "Watch that back shooter. He's crooked as a snake."

"Oh, I intend to. I know Ike—real well."

"Didn't figure that you were any dude just wandering around looking for gold sticking out of the ground. Good luck getting your horses back."

"Thanks, I'll need it before this is over."

He rode back to Jim's place and arrived after sundown. Rosa rushed out and looked at the horse he led in the stream of light from the doorway. "He's a damn nice horse."

"He's yours." He tossed her the reins.

"Oh, how nice. What's his name?" she asked.

"Call him what you want. He won't come when you call it out anyway." He laughed at her and shook his head. She gave him a frown and led the bay off to put him in the corral.

He trailed along after her. "Anything new happen here today?"

She shook her head and he stepped in to take off the saddle for her.

"I guess we'll go to the horse races and see what we can learn."

"It could be dangerous." She closed the gate behind the horse.

"Everything's dangerous." He herded her back to the house.

7

The racetrack was a dusty place in the valley. Wagons, buggies, and horseback riders were all headed for the site, churning up clouds of dirt with all their activity. Bicycle riders were weaving in and out of the crowd. Everyone was headed for the flat track. Several haciendas had their men in similar-colored clothing and leading some powerful animals that they expected to win for them. Some even had large tents for shade and shelter for the elite owners' comfort.

Slocum separated from Rosa before they reached the track area so she could spy on things. The thing he wanted to know the most was how many gunhands Ike had along with him. He might have several, but knowing Ike's recklessness—perhaps none.

All Slocum could do was hope there were only a few.

In the maze of people, vendors, and the curious, Slocum couldn't find any sign of Clanton. Jim Davis and O'Riley were to come later so that they didn't appear to be associated with him. Perhaps Clanton was coming at the last minute to get in the race, then be gone. He surely knew by this time that someone was looking for that horse.

There was something going on that caught Slocum's eyes

and ears. Someone must have arrived on the other side of the track. Several people rushed over there to see what was happening.

Slocum drifted with the movement but held back. Obviously from the commotion and the crowd's sounds, Ike was playing the big role, no doubt showing off the stallion. Two men had delivered him on lead ropes between them. Through the billowing cloud of dust, Slocum at last saw the scar on the horse's neck. The flaw that indisputably identified him.

The two men who had brought him did not look like the toughest men in the country. This shifty pair acted nervous enough that they might shoot themselves in the foot if spooked. If he'd been on horseback, he might have charged in and taken the horse while they were off guard. Ike, obviously drunk, staggered around and talked loudly about his "fucking" racehorse. Every fourth word in his speech included that word.

Slocum dropped back and went toward the tents. Behind one, he found Rosa and checked with her. She'd not seen a man in the crowd she suspected of being a Clanton guard.

"Have you seen the stallion?" she asked.

Slocum nodded and they both turned away from the dust devil that came swirling through tents and people. "It's O'Riley's horse, all right. He has the scar on his neck."

"What should we do?"

"I may jerk the jockey off him and then you and I ride for it. You think you can ride him?"

She nodded and smiled like she was ready.

"Keep me in mind."

"I will. You be careful." Then they drifted apart as casually as they could.

He needed to warn O'Riley and Jim so they were aware of his plans, as sketchy as they were at that moment. Inside the first tent, he saw servants filling glasses with wine for the privileged. Several dark-eyed, eligible daughters were surrounded by some well-dressed suitors and the fanning older chaperons close at hand to observe all that happened.

No way he could use them to distract attention from the horse. They were less than three miles from the International

Line and Arizona Territory. While the Mexicans might not recognize the theft of the horse, Arizona officials should.

He still didn't have everything worked out—but he planned to take the stallion by force and use the moment of shock to escape if there was a way. This was the least defensive place that Clanton could have him in, and that meant it was time to move.

Outside in the blazing sun again, Slocum worked his way through the milling crowd. Bets were being placed. The Ortega Hacienda had a fine gray horse. A straight Barb-bred horse that drew lots of attention. Slocum lingered around the crowd that looked over the stalwart stallion.

"No one can beat that gray ghost," some unknown man said from beside him.

Slocum agreed and then moved on.

He singled out Jim at last and they went behind a flapping tent.

"The horse is here. Don't let O'Riley do anything foolish. I'm going to try to rush in and take him. That means I won't be able to take him to your place."

Jim nodded. "What can I do?"

"Keep an eye on O'Riley. Tell him if I get the stallion I will deliver him to his man in Nogales as quick as I can."

"I can do that. You be careful."

"In the confusion here, this is the best chance we have to separate Clanton and that horse."

Jim agreed and said, "Keep your head down."

Slocum closed his gritty eyes. "I will."

The time for the race drew closer. A six-horse field was being drawn by the committee, which was composed of the hacienda owners and the drunk Clanton. They argued vocally apart from the public. Each of the teams sought ways and means to best show off their horse. Lots of respect would go to the winner and the rich Mexicans had lots of pride to spread over the rest of the populace in such meets.

The horses were paraded before the bettors and onlookers. Slocum hurried to find Rosa. At last he located her and she ran to him.

"Get your horse and be at the end of the race. Depending on how things go, be ready to either ride or lead him," he said to her.

"I am ready. I will be there."

Slocum headed for where he had hobbled the Roman-nosed gelding when he discovered that two hard-case Mexican vaqueros were shadowing him. Using the horse for a shield, he drew his handgun. The .45 in his fist, he waited behind for them to draw closer.

He stepped out and confronted them. "Did you come to kill me?"

Both men went for their guns. Slocum's Colt barked lead and death at the two. They were too slow and crumpled in the loose dirt with smoking guns in their fists. Screams went up from the shocked crowd, who turned their attention to the north edge where the gunshots had sounded, and many ran screaming for cover.

Already in the saddle, Slocum sent his upset horse for the parade of racers. He reached Clanton's shocked jockey and just about collided the bay with the stallion. With a shove, Slocum spilled the jockey out of the saddle. He drove his bay in closer and caught the reins of the Thoroughbred. He counted on the stallion to really lead and swung him around in close presence to his own stirrup, then he looked toward the blue sky horizon and the U.S. border.

He charged out and the stallion matched the bay's urgency stride for stride beside his stirrup. From across the open ground he could see Rosa coming across the field on her own horse to join him. She turned north to point the way for him. He had the big horse in his control.

Even over the crowd's protests, he could hear Clanton's hysterical screams. "Stop that fucker! He's stolen my horse."

The ground he viewed was flat toward the border with sparse clumps of greasewood and bunches of dry grass on both sides. That made the way clear, and the two of them were set to make a run for the International Line. He glanced back and nodded at Rosa's anxious look as she whipped her horse to go faster and keep up.

They needed a few precious minutes before the men with Clanton and the others recovered. They needed the time to get enough lead on the ones who would pursue them. Crossing the unattended border would not mean safety, but it was all Slocum could do in the short time ahead.

This would be a race. Both his horse and the stallion were running free, though he might need to switch to riding the stallion and the jockey saddle if he had a desperate closing with his pursuers. He looked back through the dust cloud trailing them. No sign of pursuit yet, but Ike would never stand still for the theft. They'd damn sure be coming.

8

Slocum shouted to Rosa, "Go hide at Jim's. I can outrun them now."

She nodded, pushing her new horse hard to keep up. "Be careful. Where can I meet you?"

"I'll find you," he shouted and pulled away as she went to the east.

He crossed near the International Line border markers and headed into the mountains. The trail narrowed, and leading the big horse became harder. He halted on a rise that topped the first ridge. Sweat soaked, both horses dripped as they gasped for breath, and Slocum changed his saddle to the stallion. There was dust rising from far out in the valley. No doubt the pursuit. He stepped in the stirrup and the upset stallion whirled around, but Slocum sent him uphill again through the dusty evergreen junipers, leaving his own bay horse behind.

Slocum had noticed at the stopover that the stud's hooves looked recently reshod. Good. He set him over the top of a rise and down the far slope, which was steep, but the horse was sure-footed. The trail would lead into the Mule Mountains, and if he was lucky he might shake the pursuit. It was still more than forty twisty miles to Nogales, and the delivery of the stallion was no sure deal. But Slocum intended to beat their pursuit

60

and get him there. All he needed was to remember who O'Riley said was supposed to accept him and the horse. That was the least of his worries.

The loose gravel slid under the horse's footing in places on the steep path, but the hard-breathing horse recovered quickly from his once-pampered racetrack life. Slocum reached down and patted him on the neck for his alertness to the changing situation. This big horse would do his part. Slocum needed to reach some flatter ground to let him race. Few horses could gain much time on him there. Still, there was no easy way off these hills and that would be his next mission.

The heat rose as he and King, as Slocum named him, dropped down in elevation. Slocum had no idea how far back the pursuit was. Both the height of the mountains and the dense junipers behind him made him turn in the saddle to listen closely.

He knew distance was his best chance. The rough country could thin down the number of the determined who would try to catch him. In ten more miles, only Clanton's most convinced chasers would be left. If he had time to cover the horse's hooves and leave only blurred tracks, that could make it harder for them to follow him, short of an Apache's effort. But he had no time for that, nor the material to do it.

Some goats grazing on the brush scattered at his approach. Reining in King, he nodded to the woman herding them. "Sorry, but I'm in a hurry."

She nodded. "Go with God," she said in Spanish and waved him on. He left her and hurried the stallion over some smoother place. The canyon narrowed and the road dropped into a dry wash where some seep holes contained pools of water.

Farther down the canyon, he let the horse drink and used his hand to cup of some of the clear water for himself. Then he remounted and headed downhill on a dim road that let him trot King. He could see the open country ahead where he hoped to find a road to Patagonia. That would be the closest town en route to the border city of Nogales.

With King short loping through the live oak country, he wondered if Clanton's men were still coming. A rifle would have been a handy defense weapon. Clanton wouldn't want anything to happen to the horse, so they'd not dare shoot much at him. Still, they'd be absolutely set on stopping him.

Was the horse receiver in Nogales named Moulton or Morton? Slocum couldn't remember, but the man would probably appear when he got there with the stallion. Leaning forward, he urged King to go faster. The skin on Slocum's back crawled. The thick creosote smell of greasewood was in his nose. Heat waves rose off the desert floor and made his vision of the Huachuca Mountains wavy. He pushed the big horse past the base of them.

Long after dark he reached Patagonia and stabled King. But before he put him in the stall, he and the swamper washed and rubbed him down with alcohol. Slocum let King only drink sips of water until he felt satisfied the big horse was cooled enough to drink what he wanted. No reason to let him develop colic or have an upset. Slocum slept close by on some loose hay.

Before sunup, he ate some food he bought from a vendor who squatted in the street. Then he saddled and rode on southwest. Late that day he'd be in the border town and find the prospective buyer.

He came off the hill and descended to the border town. Jacals crowded the hillside and the small checkpoints sat side by side straddling the International Line. He reined up at a stable on this side of the border, put King in a stall by himself, and set out to find some dinner.

Moments later he took a stool at the counter in a diner and ordered the special from a potbellied waitress. She acted like he was special until a big man in a suit came into the café all out of breath. He sat down beside Slocum.

"Ira Moulton," he said and offered him his hand. "I'm thinking you must be O'Riley. Is that my stallion?"

"Yes, but my name's Slocum. I'm helping out O'Riley. He and my friend Rosa are over east looking for the mare that Ike Clanton's bunch stole."

The man whistled through his teeth. "Did they steal the stallion too?"

"Yes, from the stables in Tucson."

"I wondered why it took him so long to get down here. I just got the word that someone with a great horse had stabled him. O'Riley wired me over a week ago that he was in Tucson and coming this way. He never answered any of my wires to him."

"He was with me looking for the horses."

"You must be tough. I don't know many men who messed with the Clantons and lived to talk about it."

"They're killers and all that, but maybe the old man's smart. Ike's an idiot. I left him screaming after me."

"Is the horse sound and all that?"

"Yes. I made damn sure of that. It may take a day or so for us to find the mare."

The big man under the silk-bound, brimmed hat nodded. "You work for O'Riley?"

"No, he couldn't afford me full-time. I'm doing this as piece-work."

"Come work for me. I can afford you." He twisted on the stool and looked Slocum up and down. "You may not be impressed, but anyone steals a horse back from the Clantons needs to work for me."

"No, thanks. I need to get back and find the mare."

"Take a day of rest. Come down to my hacienda and we'll have a few drinks, get you some pussy, and you can sleep in tomorrow."

"Sounds like heaven. You leave that invite open. I get that mare, I'll be back and take you up on it. Give me a receipt for the horse's delivery and how you will pay O'Riley for him."

"You don't trust me?"

"I trust you fine. But it ain't my money."

Moulton nodded in approval. "I understand. You're very thorough."

The man found a piece of paper in an inside coat pocket and wrote on the back of the letter the amount and the fact he had not paid the agreed price to Slocum but would do so on O'Riley's demand.

"I'd sure like the mare too," Moulton added.

Slocum put the letter in his vest pocket. "We'll work on it

next. I need to borrow a good horse. I'll return it with the mare. I had to leave mine behind after I stole King from Ike just before the races."

Moulton laughed. "I can see him red faced now. I bet he screamed at your back."

"Like a pig caught under a gate."

"I have a fine horse you can keep when you finish dinner. One of my men will deliver it here to you."

"Thanks, but I only want to borrow him."

The man shook his head to dismiss his concern about the gift. "Does O'Riley even know who he's hired?"

"I don't think so, but I almost felt sorry for him when I met him in Diamond City, and I damn sure hate Ike Clanton, who, I suspect, was behind the theft in the first place."

"That makes two of us who hate Ike."

Slocum never asked him why, but from the sound of Moulton's comment it told him that the man was no fan of the oldest son at Old Man Clanton's casa.

9

On the good horse that Moulton supplied and pushing him hard, Slocum made it back to Jim Davis's ranch two nights later sometime past midnight. Barely dressed, Rosa came on the run under the stars.

"You're back. Where is the horse?"

"In Nogales with his new owner."

"You got him there?" O'Riley shouted, busting outside and still fastening his pants.

"Yes. I have a receipt for him." He handed the paper to O'Riley and hugged Rosa's form to his left hip.

"Oh! Thank God." O'Riley crossed himself and looked to the stars.

"Hell's bells," Jim said, coming with a lamp. "Sounds like you baked the cake."

"I got lucky, my friend."

"Are you hungry?" Rosa asked.

"I'd eat something simple."

"We can fix you something," she said, hugged him, and then tore loose to rush for the house.

"O'Riley, put his horse up. The victor has come home."

"You get any problems from Ike?" he asked Jim as they headed for the house.

"Naw. Your Roman-nosed horse even made it home."

"Good. I'll have see that Moulton's horse gets back to him. Any word on the mare?"

"We think Ike's got her hidden somewhere. I was in Tombstone all day talking to folks who know about things. There ain't a word leaked out, and that's strange."

"How is that?"

"Hell, someone from Clanton's bunch usually gets loose tongued on liquor and spills the beans. There ain't a word about the mare."

"We may need to put Ike's balls in a vise." Slocum smiled at his friend.

"What are you planning to do?" O'Riley asked, coming back inside the small house a lot more enthused than Slocum had seen him at anytime previous.

Slocum glanced up at him in the lamplight. "We've got to find the mare next."

"Where can we start?" O'Riley asked.

"I'm not sure, but we may need to find someone close to Ike and notch his ears until he tells us where he's hid the mare."

Rosa put a platter on the table with the eggs, fried side meat, and reheated biscuits. The smell of the fresh breakfast ran up Slocum's nose and reminded him how hungry he was. Saliva flooded from behind his lower teeth and he took up his fork to eat. The taste burst in his mouth at the first bite and he smiled at her. "Damn good."

She nodded and he could see how anxious she was to be closer to him, but she restrained herself, sitting back from the two men. Later he could give her the attention she needed. Her body, he decided, would be a great sweet desert after the meal.

"Where do we need to start?" Jim asked. "By damn, I want to help you two get this matter settled."

"Tomorrow. We'll cut out a couple of his hired men and rough them up if we need to, to find out where he's stuck that mare."

O'Riley nodded. "I've never been tough in my life, but they have me so mad. I could get mean on them."

"Good, it looks like we're going to have to be."

"Where we going first?"

"Tombstone."

"You figure we can head some of them off short of there?" Jim asked.

Slocum shook his head. "No, I want them coming back from there."

Jim nodded. "Riding back home, all liquored up. Good idea."

"We'll need to be up there in a few hours to catch some of them."

"Grab the light. We'll go saddle the horses," O'Riley said. He and Jim left Slocum and Rosa alone.

"You aren't going to go, are you?" Rosa asked, frowning with concern at him. In a swish of her skirt, she was against him, keeping him seated. "Let them go do it."

"I want this damn business over. The stallion is at Moulton's and we need the mare there as well, then we can do whatever the hell we want to do."

She leaned close to his ear. "I really need you, but I understand. You should realize that you are tired and may not be quick enough —"

He hugged her to him. "I can handle myself. I'll be back."

She swallowed hard. "I plan to go along. I won't get in the way."

He agreed and got to his feet. "We'll find her."

"I just want you to be careful. Ike Clanton is a rattlesnake."

He herded her toward the outside and kissed her in the doorway. Jim Davis came back for his rifle and told them so.

"Good idea."

The main track from Tombstone to Old Man Clanton's ranch was the road that came by Davis's front gate. They'd saddled the Roman-nosed horse for Slocum. He acted fresh and rowdy, but once in the saddle, Slocum never let him buck on their way to the entrance gate.

In the lead, Slocum short loped his horse for the pass up on the hill where they could see any riders coming back from town under the stars. The horses were soon hidden out of sight and

O'Riley was assigned to watch the road while Slocum caught some shut-eye on top of a bedroll that Rosa had spread out for him. The others rested, seated nearby in a grassy spot beside the road in the greasewood.

Slocum felt like he'd only slept ten minutes when Rosa woke him. "Three men are coming."

"Good." He stood up and checked his Colt out of habit. It was half-cocked, and he rolled the cylinder on his sleeve, looking at it in the dim light with care. Satisfied, he closed the gate and reset the empty under the hammer.

"Hold up!" Jim shouted and used a rifle shot to punctuate his order. In the confusion, the riders' horses bumped into each other and unseated one rider. Cussing filled the night.

"Get off those horses." Slocum was there. He caught the downed man by his collar and stood him on his feet with the six-gun in his right fist.

"You sonsabitches—" His words were cut short when Slocum busted him over the shoulder with his gun butt and he crumpled to his knees, screaming in pain.

Slocum gave the man's butt a boot and sent him sprawling on his face in the dust. "Shut your mouth and stay there."

The third man threw his hands up higher, and O'Riley jerked his six-gun out of its holster. Jim held the rifle muzzle on them.

"Where is the stolen race mare?" Slocum demanded.

The one on his feet shook his head. "How should I know?"

"Someone better know or I'm going to notch your ears until I hear the answer." He holstered his six-gun. Then the blade of his large jackknife glinted in the starlight after he opened it. "Who's first?"

"The damn mare ain't at the ranch," the cusser said.

"You guys live on that ranch. There ain't nothing happens down there that you don't know about. That mare was there and taken someplace else. One of you knows and I'm going to notch your ears one at a time until you tell me where she's at."

"He—he sold her," the least ruffled one said.

"To who?"

"Some Mexican bandit."

The one massaging his head said in disgust, "He's telling you the damn truth."

"What's his name?" Slocum demanded. "The Mexican bandit."

"Pico is all we know."

Slocum glanced at Rosa and she nodded.

No wonder Pico's woman didn't want them to search the place. The mare might be in the mountains or anywhere. The man was a shrewd trader by his reputation and he might have had a buyer if he knew anything about her pedigree.

Rosa had gathered the Clanton men's horses.

"What should we do with them?" Jim asked.

Slocum nodded as the others got to their feet. "I can't tell you what to do, but Old Man Clanton don't like informers. He learns that you gave us answers, your health may suffer."

"Can we leave?" the sassy one asked.

"Without your guns," Slocum said.

They grumbled and mounted up. Their chosen direction was north toward Tombstone. They'd picked the road back. Clanton might never learn what they'd told Slocum about the mare's whereabouts.

"What's next?" O'Riley asked.

"We better ride to the mountains." Slocum drew a deep breath. When they finally found and delivered that mare, he intended to sleep for a week. He took the reins from Rosa. "We need to go back to the house and prepare to head back up there."

The pink on the far horizon told him that it would soon be sunup. He boosted Rosa into the saddle. The same question kept going by—is that mare up there in the clouds? In two days they'd know the answer to that important question.

"I worry about you," Rosa whispered.

He shook his head. They rode hard for the ranch. His eyes burned in the first golden light that speared the valley coming over the Chiricahuas. The Roman-nosed horse was a much harder ride than King or the borrowed horse. Before this matter was over he'd probably have a showdown with Clanton or some of his men. *Bring them on*, he thought. He wanted this matter cleared up.

After getting supplies at the ranch, they rode on for Mexico. Slocum rocked in the saddle; he should have changed horses and left the Roman-nosed gelding back at the ranch. It would be a long day's ride on this stiff-legged gelding.

10

They reached Los Nigra under the cover of night. Rosa found them food at her grandmother's jacal. When everyone else was bedded down in hammocks, she led Slocum to a side room and they undressed. Stolen kisses encouraged their growing needs. His boots were toed off. Skirt strings were untied, revealing a flash of her slender brown legs in the starlight that spilled in through the open window. The cooler night mountain air sought their exposed skin as they snuggled together, deeply involved in the foreplay growing between them. Mouth to mouth, their needs flared like fireworks. Swept up in flames, he sought her most intimate organ and penetrated her with a fiery sword that took her breath away. Her contractions soon swallowed his sword to the depths. Lightning struck his genitals and they cramped, squeezing out lavalike eruptions into her belly.

Their breath gone, their energy depleted, they lay connected as the liquids of their lovemaking oozed out. Like precious gold, drop by drop the fluids escaped. They went to sleep in each other's arms.

Rosa was up before sunrise. Slocum awoke in the darkness, felt around for her, and discovered only the warm spot under the covers. In a few moments, wearing his pants, he found a dark corner in the yard and emptied his bladder. Walking back on bare feet, he grabbed his shirt off the chair and went to find her in the kitchen.

She was busy scrambling eggs and making flour tortillas. Her mixture of pork and peppers sizzled on the black grill.

"Stir my meat," she said when he came in the room.

He moved over and used a flipper to turn it over with a sizzle. The rich aroma of food filled the air and her coffee perked. "Thanks, we need to get riding."

"Get the others up," she said, taking up another large tortilla. Then she started another on the grill.

He agreed and went to wake Davis and O'Riley. In the cool mountain air, he rocked each hammock, and the occupants awoke with moans. The mood of his helpers was strained. Amused, Slocum smiled and went back to get some of the fresh coffee. No sympathy for his men.

"What if the mare isn't up here?" Rosa asked when he came over and squeezed her shoulder.

"We look other places. Someone knows where she is and we'll find her."

"'Cause you always win?"

He smiled. "Not always, but I really try."

"At about anything you do." She elbowed him and laughed like she knew the facts.

"That too." He began to fill the cups set out on the counter.

Davis came in and took one of the steaming cups with a nod. "By God, you're a lucky man to have her."

"I am."

"So you know it."

O'Riley yawned, entering the room. "Smells good. I can't believe you don't have a husband, Rosa."

"Maybe she did have one," Slocum said, amused. "And she poisoned him."

Davis about broke up at the scowl that she cast at Slocum. The rancher had to turn to hide his snickering amusement.

Slocum stood before her and winked. She dismissed his words with a head shake and gave him two plates full of food. "I'll bring the rest."

After the meal, they saddled the horses to start for the mountains. Slocum asked Rosa where her cousin and grandmother were.

"They went to see Grandmama's oldest daughter. She may be dying, they fear."

He nodded and booted the gelding on up the steep grade. By midday they approached Pico's ranch. He had wondered during the entire trip over the mountain whether the man's sassy wife would be there and what she would do. It made no matter; it just made him uncomfortable to have to handle a sorry bitch like her in the first place.

"How are we going to do this?" Davis asked.

"They may shoot at us this time, especially if they have the mare. Rosa, you stay up here."

She shook her head. "You are going, so am I."

He shook his head at her decision, but had no way to enforce his wishes. He turned back to O'Riley and Jim. "It comes to them shooting at us, be prepared to duck or shoot back."

"I don't have a gun," O'Riley said.

Slocum nodded that he heard him. What use would O'Riley have for one? He didn't know how to use one. Besides, he might shoot one of them by mistake.

"Jim and I will handle the shooting part."

The man agreed.

At the ranch gate, they rode four abreast toward the house. Those at the ranch headquarters wouldn't discover that half of Slocum's group were unarmed until they were close enough to see them, and then it should be too late to do much.

Tight lipped, Slocum nodded at Rosa and whispered, "Be prepared to get out of the way if hell breaks loose."

Pico's wife busted out of the log cabin and screeched, "What the hell do you want this time?"

"A horse you're concealing."

"I don't have your gawdamn horse."

"Then you have no worries."

She went to pointing for them to get out, but Slocum never let his horse halt. "O'Riley, you go around and look in her corrals."

Pale under his freckles, he swallowed hard, then set his horse out to do as he was ordered.

"Is your husband here?" Slocum asked, believing that if Pico were there, he'd have come out to meet them.

"That's none of your damn business either." Her hands were set defiantly on her hips, and her dark eyes glared like knives ready to cut them down.

O'Riley rode back around and shook his head, still looking unsure of himself.

Slocum said over his shoulder. "Jim, go ride the pasture and look some more. I think she's concealing that mare somewhere."

"I'll go with him," Rosa said after riding up close to Slocum.

He agreed and asked their hostess, "When's Ike been up here last?"

She shook her head. "Ike's never been here."

"That's a lie."

"Well, he may want to kill you when he hears you have been bothering me."

"That's nice. Ike is too big a coward to even threaten me." He shook his head in disgust.

She stamped her foot. "His men aren't."

"Thanks for the warning." When he heard the returning hoofbeats, he turned to O'Riley. "They're bringing a horse. Be sure that it's yours."

His green eyes flew open wide when Jim loped around the house with a lariat encircling the neck of a tall mare. Rosa herded her.

"That's my mare." O'Riley looked at the bay in shocked disbelief. "That's her."

Slocum glared at Pico's wife. "They hang horse thieves, lady."

She glared back at him. "You won't get away with this."

"Hanging you? Oh, yes, we can." He had no intention of lynching her, but he should have.

Standing in the saddle, Jim reached over and fashioned a halter on the mare's nose. Rosa nodded in approval.

"Oh, thank God," O'Riley said and crossed himself.

"Let's go," Slocum said, wanting to head west in case they had someone on their back trail.

"Where are we going?" O'Riley asked when they started to leave.

Slocum waved away his question. He rode closer to Pico's woman. "Next time, I will hang you."

Arms folded, she spat at him defiantly.

He considered whipping her with the reata on his saddle. No way she was worth that, so he reined the horse around to take the lead. They rode out and headed westward.

Once they were out of hearing range, Slocum said, "There may be someone following us. We'll go off the west slopes and head for Nogales with the mare."

Jim agreed, looking around. "I wonder where the hell her husband was today."

"He don't stay home much," Slocum teased.

"I wouldn't either." The rancher shook his head at him.

"How far are we from Nogales?" O'Riley asked.

"We can't go the shortest, easy route. Clanton's men will be ready for us there. So we'll have to go through the Madres. It'll take a lot longer than the shortest route, but it's our best bet to get the horse there without trouble. Five or six hard days. When we get off the far side of the Madres, we'll have some tough desert to cover."

"Isn't that dangerous?" O'Riley asked.

"We don't have much choice. If Ike figured we were headed up here, he might have sent several pistoleros this way to stop us and recover the mare."

"I never figured it would be this damn hard to get two horses to the man who purchased them."

"Your ignorance of the West is why."

Slocum pushed his horse to the lead. Riding up through the pines, he heard a harpy eagle souring overhead. His screams threatened them for their trespassing in his kingdom.

"He don't like us being here," Slocum said.

"That's easy to tell." Rosa laughed.

The high elevation soon began to tell on horses and riders. They rested on a small shelf. Having no food or supplies with them might prove to be the biggest challenge for his team, and having to hunt would slow them down too.

"Jim, if you see a deer, we need to shoot it."

The rancher agreed, sitting on his butt, hugging his knees. "I'll watch for one."

"Right," Slocum said. "We should spook up one today."

Then Slocum turned to O'Riley. "What are you going to do, O'Riley, when you get this mare to Nogales?"

"Get the hell out of this spiny country and back where I belong." He had his straw hat off and ran his fingers through his uncombed hair. "I sure don't belong out here."

Slocum nodded he'd heard him. He'd known O'Riley didn't belong in the West when he'd met him in Diamond City. "You going to go look for your wife?"

"No. That bitch can earn her own living in a whorehouse."

"Don't her folks have money?"

"Yeah, but when I tell them what she did to me they'll dis-own her."

"Blood's thicker than you think. She may have already made up a story about you abandoning her."

O'Riley shook his shoulders in revulsion. "That bitch may have. She lied to me that she was pregnant, then she had a period on our honeymoon. She's worthless."

Rosa winked at Slocum and said, "He has had such a bad life out here."

Slocum rose slowly. "Time to move on. We should reach the pass and be on the western slopes by sundown."

They mounted with effort and moved out. Hard to be more than wishful that this trying trip would finally be over when they reached Nogales. Slocum knew they had many miles to cover to even get there.

Slocum downed a yearling black-tailed deer, and they cut its throat and slung it over Jim's lap until they found water to dress it. They crossed the pass over the high point and dropped down the other side. The distant scene showed the desert far to the west a hazy view.

In a few hours, they found a good spring and stopped for the night. The deer carcass was hung on some low limbs of a pine and they quickly skinned it, then removed the intestines.

The liver set aside for eating, they cleaned out the deer and washed it down with water.

Jim and O'Riley gathered the dry wood for a fire. When Slocum and Rosa had the dressing completed, she started the fire to cook supper as the sun slipped off into the faraway Gulf of California.

They ate hearty since they had no way to keep the rest of the uneaten meat from spoiling after a couple of days. That would be days short of their destination. In the morning they ate lots more of the cooked deer's haunches and rode on.

The trail proved steep and in many places they were forced to dismount and walk their animals past some challenging precipices. Crossing flats of pine forest, their tense muscles relaxed and they laughed, though still with a twang of anxiousness in the sounds.

"Have you been over this route before?" O'Riley asked Slocum at a stop to rest the animals.

"I have been over several trails in these mountains. Not necessarily this particular trail, but this one will lead us to the way down."

O'Riley nodded that he'd heard him.

They traveled hard all day. In late afternoon, they found water and grass for the horses in an open meadow locked in the mountain vastness. Numb from the long excursion, they ate more cooked meat and sat in silence. With enough venison left for their morning meal, they dropped off to sleep early and woke before sunrise in the chill of the high elevation.

Saddled and ready, they went on after finding a more heavily used trail in midmorning. Slocum felt relieved and knew the way off the Madres from this position.

He looked over the train and nodded. "We're on a good way down."

The nods of his companions followed.

Midafternoon, the rumble of thunder spread overhead as an afternoon monsoon shower began to grow. Soon icy drops pelted them. They huddled in their saddles, moving on with little problem but lots of discomfort for everyone and the horses.

The clouds broke up near sundown and the sparkling look of water droplets shone on the pine needles like diamonds. Cold to the bone, they shivered and pushed their horses on. They'd be out of the Madres in another day, then they'd face the desert. That would be hot going after shedding the coolness of the heights.

At sundown he told them this would be a dry stopover. The next water was several hours away and in the darkness he didn't want to continue any farther. "Everyone needs to wipe their horse's muzzle with a wet rag, and you can chew on some jerky Jim found in his saddle bags."

Santa Maria was less then thirty miles away. There they could buy supplies and a pack animal or two. He'd be glad when they reached the small settlement. The risk he'd taken over going west had worked so far. But the desert would nonetheless be a real challenge too.

He enjoyed Rosa's willingness to share her womanhood with him in the bedroll. The last draining moments sent him into deep sleep to arise from in the morning's coolest hours. When everyone was awake and saddled up, they moved on to the next wet spot.

The stone water tanks at the Holy Waters came into view like a miracle. Towering gnarled cottonwoods rustled in the hot midday winds. Slocum dismounted, warning the rest not to let their animals drink too much. "Only a small amount, then drag them away. We don't need any colicky horses."

After he let his mount drink, he swung back into the saddle. "I'm going into Santa Maria after some supplies, and I'll be back in a few hours. Keep your guard up. There are lots of bandits around here."

Jim nodded that he understood. In fact he was the only armed one in camp and Slocum hated to leave him, but he didn't want to expose his team and the mare to the curious eyes for very long in the desperate region where this settlement sat.

He found the village and mission quiet. He stopped at the large mercantile and went in to buy supplies. Two young clerks waited on him as he rattled off the things he'd need.

"What about two sound mules to pack this?"

The two boys looked at each other. The older one said he knew about two such animals for sale with packsaddles.

"How much?"

"Forty dollars for the two."

"Go buy them." He put the money on the counter. This was not the time to dicker a deal on them. "If they're good, I'll pay both of you a dollar apiece."

They smiled and nodded, and the older boy said, "They are good mules. I will go get them."

"Good. Load them. I will be back in a few hours for them."

"*Sí*, señor."

He bought a sackful of tamales from a vendor and rode back to camp. They scrambled to their feet, brushing off their butts and then hurrying over.

"Have some tamales," he said, handing Rosa the cloth bag to dole them out. "I bought two pack mules and supplies that should get us to Nogales."

"See any threat?" Jim asked, peeling the corn shuck off his food.

Slocum shook his head. "But our supplies and mules will be reported to every evil person in the area. I say we take the mules and ride far from here tonight."

Rosa nodded. O'Riley shook his head in disgust, but in the end agreed it was best for them to go on.

Twilight had set in when they collected the saddled and packed mules. Jim and Rosa checked them over while Slocum went inside with O'Riley to settle his bill with the store. With the merchandise and mules paid for, the store owner thanked them and told them to come back.

When Slocum came out of the store, Jim told him that the packsaddles were secure. In the dimming light of day, they mounted up and rode on out.

When they reached a high point, Slocum looked back at the village being swallowed by dusk and wondered how many would-be bandits knew about their presence in the region. Like buzzards looking for carrion, such men would search for them. Simply moving on was not enough; they needed to push hard to deliver the mare.

They rode hard for a while, but finally had to stop for a few hours' sleep. Before dawn they all climbed back in the saddle, still half asleep. Slocum wanted to get to Nogales as soon as possible, and many miles of desert still separated them from the final delivery spot.

Heat and long days were taking their toll on the three men, one woman, and their animals, and they hadn't been riding as hard as Slocum had hoped to. They grained their horses and mules morning and night to ensure they had the energy they needed.

The next night, they rested at an abandoned hacienda and bathed in a warm, mossy tank to shed some of the grit and grime that chafed every crease in their bodies. The freshness of their cleaned skin rejuvenated them into riding harder the next two days.

At San Mateo, they stayed at a well-guarded hacienda. An old friend of Slocum's, José Demaria, showed them his hospitality and flirted with Rosa like a young man anxious to steal her. Slocum could see how flattering Rosa found his friend's attentions. After a short rest and clean clothes, she danced gracefully with the gray-haired *patrón*, sliding across the tile floor of the great room to strumming guitar music.

They joined Demaria for a fancy supper that evening and even O'Riley acted awake. A night's sleep in a good bed with no fears of attack lifted the stress they had borne out in the brittle desert.

"Let us toast my great friend Slocum for our longtime friendship." Demaria was on his feet to toast him with a glass of wine.

Everyone rose and Rosa squeezed Slocum's arm. "Isn't he a wonderful man to do that for you?"

Slocum agreed and the cheers went up as he rose to his feet. He and Demaria went back a long ways in some wars with Mexican *bandidos* that had stretched over several years.

"The death of those warlords made my region safe for all the people to live here."

Slocum nodded and hoisted his glass. Then they sat down

and ate their meal. Rosa bubbled to him about the spacious casa and their host.

Their bedroom had a high bed in the center of the room set on a platform with carpeted stairs. In the heavenly featherbed, Slocum squeezed and kissed Rosa. She threw back her head to kiss him. "You are a wonderment to bring us to this marvelous haven."

Before they left the next day, Demaria warned Slocum there was information coming to him that Ike Clanton planned to stop Slocum's delivery near the border. Slocum acknowledged his words. "Ike is a cowardly braggart. He'll send some of his tough pistoleros to meet us."

After so many days of hard-pressed traveling, his small band was still two days short of the delivery point. Slocum hoped they were sharp enough to cover their movements. Jim and Slocum scouted way ahead. Their plans were to enter the United States at the Peralta Springs Ranch, still a long way from Nogales.

Jim had gone in and warned the guards that they would be coming in hard.

Slocum waited until dark to cross the last open miles of desert to the ranch headquarters. The ranch employees were heavily armed against the Apaches, who regularly crisscrossed the line coming and going to the Sierra Madres. He wanted to be certain they knew he was not an Apache.

As Jim had warned the Peraltas, Slocum's group rode in without any delay, unsure of what they'd find.

The *segundo* for the Peraltas, Juan Calero, met them wearing a crossbelt of ammunition and armed with a Winchester rifle. He asked, "Have you seen those damn Cowboys?"

Slocum dismounted, shook his head, and then shook the man's hand. "We haven't seen any sign of them. Are they around here now?"

Calero nodded. "Come, we have beds for you and your men—and your woman too."

"Do you expect the Cowboys to attack you?" Slocum asked once the others had been led off.

"I have the word that they have orders to get the mare back at any cost."

Slocum shook his head. "She's only a good mare."

With a serious frown, Calero nodded in the lamplight. "You have made that whole Clanton family mad."

"I couldn't care less about those bastards. We need to deliver her," Slocum said. "What I need now is a buckboard and your Gatling gun to mow them down with."

"Oh, I could not loan you that gun." Calero shook his head. "The *patrón* would be very upset."

"Just an idea. It could whittle down Clanton's forces in short order."

Calero agreed, then told one of his guardsmen to show him to his quarters. "They won't get you here, señor."

"Thank you," Slocum said. His suggestion to the man had not been accepted. Oh well, it was only a notion.

"You are safe here. We have that Gatling gun and it works well."

Clanton's men damn sure would never charge a Gatling gun. Slocum went off to join Rosa in a small jacal. He thanked his guide and slipped through the curtain over the doorway and into the room. When she looked up, a small lamp on a stand illuminated Rosa's face where she sat on the bed.

"I'm sorry," Slocum told her. "This business has been hell. We are a day or more from delivering the mare and having it over with."

"But they say that Clanton and his gang will track you down and kill you."

"Aw, they've got better things to do than that." He shook his head to dismiss her concern.

She hugged him tight. "I don't want anything to happen to you."

He patted her back and squeezed her. "They aren't getting me. You'll see."

"When will we leave?"

"In the morning. I will talk to Calero before we leave."

With her slender body pressed hard against him, he realized that she needed some attention. The past few hectic days had offered little opportunity for them to be private enough to have much of a sexual exchange. He bent over and kissed her, and her hot tongue sought his mouth. In their hurry to get to each other, they undressed with their mouths engaged. He undid the gun belt and tossed the rig on the bed. Then he toed off his boots, still kissing her mouth hard.

She untied her skirt, let it fall, and stepped clear of it. They separated and she took the blouse off over her head. His hands cupped her firm breasts and she smiled as he felt and tested them. Then he stepped out of his pants and shoved them down. His arms swept her up to carry her over to the bed.

"I'll try not to drop you on my holster."

She laughed and hugged his head. "That wouldn't even hurt me."

"It might," he said, easing her down, then taking the gun belt off the bed. He buckled and hung it on the rung of the ladder-back chair. He came back and put his knee on the bed as she held out her arms.

When Slocum was settled between her raised legs, she lifted herself up enough to capture his erection in her fist and pull him inside her vagina. Saliva flowed in his mouth, forcing him to swallow as he pushed his dick inside of her. The way was slick and tight. Obviously she was worked up enough to really make things smoke between them.

She raised her butt to accept all she could and he went to pounding her ass. His brain swirled, and his breath came harder, and his hips complained the deeper and faster they went. Then she stiffened, straining under him, and he knew she had come. Bleary-eyed, she closed her lashes again as he filled her with his seminal fluid. She slid off into never-never land.

He remained inside her, braced on his arms, and waited for her to awake.

At last she sighed. "I am in heaven."

"Not exactly. But you are sweet."

"Will we ever get the mare to Nogales?"

He fondled her left breast and winked in the dark at her. "That's what we hired on to do. Somehow we will do that."

She pushed her small butt at him, moving his still-half-stiff dick deeper inside her. "You going to do something about him?" She meant his hard-on.

"Darling, I can't wait."

She rose up and kissed him on the lips. "Good."

He shoved his stem deeper into her vagina and felt his dick respond after the fourth probe. His heart rate began to speed up. The shaft turned to iron and his mouth flooded with saliva. As he headed toward more pleasure, his strokes grew stronger and she returned his actions. Her heels began to beat the backs of his legs. Her juices lubricated their way, and both of them were breathing like racehorses. The swollen head of his dick and the first few inches of his length expanded hard and tight, ready to explode. Farther back the friction on his stick made him itch with a desire for more action.

A crushing pain shot through his gonads and the connecting cords strained to rocket the fiery volcanic semen out through the swollen head of his cock and deep inside her body.

"Oh, I felt that." She gasped and closed her eyes, collapsing underneath him.

"You were made for this," he whispered in her ear, pumping her easy-like and savoring her tightness and the soft clenching inside still coming from her muscular walls.

"Thank God I got to know you, hombre." Her arms squeezed him tight and he fired off a lesser blast in final response.

"Will we leave early tomorrow?" she asked after he climbed off and left her lying on her back beside him.

"Yes. I may hire a few of Calero's men to get us through the Mule Mountains. He can loan us a few tough men to get us that far. Then we can make a run for it."

She clapped his chest. "A good plan."

He nodded.

Would it be enough?

11

Peralta's hacienda man agreed with Slocum. He'd loan him four of his best men.

"What if we took the Gatling gun?"

"My *patrón* might kill me if they raid us and we don't have that gun here." Calero's face under the lamplight looked concerned. Then he laughed. "You take it. Hope those bastards do try to jump you. You will uncover that damn gun with a canvas and mow them down. Yes, I will select the men to ride with you past the Mule Mountains."

"What will we owe you?"

"Nothing, but you may pay my men for helping you. And, Slocum—"

"Yes?"

"Don't you let anyone steal my big gun."

"I understand." He went to tell Jim and O'Riley what he'd set up.

Some of the ranch women were feeding his crew breakfast. A handsome woman in her forties brought him some coffee and a plate of food piled high.

"Is my crazy husband coming?" she asked with a small smile at the corner of her soft mouth.

Slocum nodded, then in a low voice drew his team in close.

"We will have four pistoleros that will ride guard with us across the Mule Mountains."

"I can hire six good men in Tombstone to guard us the rest of the way." Jim said. "Let me go and hire them."

"Be damn careful. We will need you on that next leg of the trip."

"I can get through and I'll meet you at the western base of the mountains."

Slocum caught his sleeve and pulled him down to whisper in his ear. "I will have the Gatling gun too."

Jim broke out laughing and shaking his head. He finished his plate, thanked the lady in charge, and went for his horse.

Slocum met Jim outside, and they both agreed they had a real chance to get through. The food had been as good as the news about Calero's help to get them over the mountains.

Taking the route along the border side of the mountains would have been easier, but that path would run right into Clanton's lap. Slocum had no intention of doing that despite the steep pass and canyon country they would have to cross instead.

Fernando was Calero's man in charge. A burly man for a Mexican, with a bushy black mustache, he was the picture of a fighting man. Contra was the gunner of his men, a small man, but fierce. Raphael was a short, thickset pistolero, and Juarez was part Indian and more thinly built. Those tough veterans were as good as having a company of soldiers, especially since they were armed with the big weapon.

In a half hour, they left the hacienda, and the horses pulling the buckboard were stout enough to be a stagecoach team. Raphael drove them; Contra rode in back. The other two pistoleros rode good ranch horses. Rosa led the two mules and the mare. O'Riley came along at the back, and he looked perkier than Slocum had ever seen him.

Fernando rode alongside Slocum as they crossed the greasewood flats. "That big gun will mow them down if they try to charge us."

"It can," Slocum agreed.

A smile crossed the man's dark face. "And they don't know what we have hidden under the canvas?"

"I doubt it. But they will learn in a damn hurry if they try us."

O'Riley nodded like he understood. "Revealing that will be a big surprise for some border bandits on the prowl, won't it?"

"Exactly," Slocum said.

"How did you figure that out?" O'Riley frowned at him.

"I fought in the Civil War. When you don't have anything else, firepower wins."

O'Riley shook his head. "I was too young, but my brother was killed fighting in it."

"Where?"

"Pennsylvania."

Slocum shook his head. "Bad place to die."

"I can't think of any place to die as good."

"Profound, the most profound thing you've said this whole time, since I met you in Diamond City."

"What will you do after we get the mare delivered?"

"Move on." Slocum blinked his eyes at the withering heat waves beginning to curtain the mountains ahead of them.

"What will you do with her?" O'Riley asked, nodding at Rosa.

"Whatever she wants to do."

"Take her along with you?"

"My life is not made for a wife. Is that what you wanted to know?"

O'Riley nodded. "Thanks, just asking."

"I recall you told me she was too expensive."

O'Riley made an uncertain head shake. "Maybe I've changed my mind. I would treat her nice. Maybe better than I did the last one."

"I'm certain it would take your best behavior to ever convince her. She'll not be easily persuaded."

"I kinda know that," O'Riley agreed.

Slocum nodded, then he dropped back to check on her. "You and this train making it?"

"Sure." A grin flashed on her face as if she felt proud he even asked.

When he looked over her wards, the mare and pack mules, he gave her a confident nod of approval. "We have some tough hours ahead, but we'll be fine with these pistoleros and that big gun."

"What will you do after we deliver the mare?"

"I'd like to find those three that raped your cousin. I'd put an ice pick through their ears to their brains."

"Will you ever find them?" She stood in the stirrups to stretch her legs.

"Someday, maybe."

"Where will you go after that? You are not one to stay long anywhere, are you?"

He agreed. "Old enemies trail me."

She nodded, then stretched her arms over her head. "I will be very sad if we must part."

He shook his head to dismiss her concerns. "We will have good memories."

She agreed, flexing some more to work out the stiffness in her muscles.

The lead mule used her movements for a chance to spook a little. In an instant she caught his lead. "Stay here, you crazy bastard. Apaches will eat you otherwise."

Slocum laughed, then booted his horse out to check on Fernando. The Clantons probably would not try anything until they were in the mountains. He planned to ask the big man's opinion about the possibility of the Clantons charging their party. He short loped Spook to catch the big man.

Ike, where the hell are you at?

12

They'd heard no word about the Clantons when his entourage started down from the head of the deep canyon that dropped off into the faraway valley. Back among the junipers that forested the mountains, Slocum and Fernando sat on their mounts and peered down the descent.

"You think if they try anything, it will be down on the flats?" Slocum asked.

"Be about the only way they can hold us up."

"I know that place. The spot where drivers rest the stage horses, halfway up the steep grade."

"Okay. We need to be ready. My men are."

"Good."

Fernando gave his driver the go-ahead wave, and they went off the top. "We will see."

Slocum agreed, jerked the repeating Winchester out of his scabbard, and balanced the butt on his leg, then sent Spook on his way. The steep side of the gravel perch—actually more of a trail than a road—plunged off the hill in a wild, twisting, downward spiral. The powerful team hitched to the wagon kept the pace to a stiff walk and, like a tortoise, moved downward under good control with the driver using the brake on the hind wheels.

Slocum told Rosa to get behind the wagon if and when the attack started. And at any expense she was not to lose the mare. She agreed and followed behind the wagon's tailgate with her three animals on leads.

In a short while they reached the flats. One minute they were listening to some quail whit-wooing and the next came "Yee-ha!" in the scream of attackers pouring from the side canyon. They heard the drum of hooves and the shouts of their riders, and the charge was on.

Slocum stepped off his horse and ran to see past the juniper cover from the edge of the wagon, with the vehicle turned broadside. One of the men jerked off the canvas from the oily smelling gun, and the muzzle swung to the right. The shots from the riders ceased when they tried to rein up their horses at the sight of the polished gun mounted in the wagon. But the deadly Gatling began to chatter, raking off riders and downing horses in a veil of smoke that surrounded the wagon.

The shrill screams of wounded men and their pained mounts as they struggled to escape the hot lead were all enveloped in a cloud of dust as man and beast alike were systematically cut down with each loud burping report of the gun.

"Alto! Alto!" Fernando shouted for his shooter to stop shooting.

Slocum could see that Rosa, the mare, and the wide-eyed mules were all right, as was O'Riley under his big straw sombrero, though the Irishman was very pale-faced and gripped his reins in equally white hands.

Slocum joined Fernando, and the two of them methodically dispatched the wounded and suffering horses. Others were dead in piles on the ground, and the other two Peralta men not manning the gun joined in disarming the Cowboys who had not escaped or died. A bloody mess. Five were dead, and four more were wounded. Slocum doubted a few of them would even survive the trip to Tombstone, but they'd send for help.

"Gracias," Slocum said to the Peralta men, shaking their hands. "I don't think they'll try that again. Tell your boss I appreciate your help. We will ride on for Nogales."

Fernando laughed. "Ah, we always wanted to use that damn

gun on them rustling no-accounts. Today that old bastard will know how deadly it is."

"I'll get word to send help for these others." Slocum motioned toward the moaning wounded, then stepped into the stirrup and rode Spook over to Rosa and O'Riley. "Let's go meet Jim."

They nodded solemnly and the column rode off the mountain, less the Peralta men's help. Shortly afterward Jim came up the road from the junction with several men to meet them. Slocum asked if they had heard the fight.

"We were coming to help you. Did you have Peralta's big gun?" Jim asked.

"Not a word—I don't want Calero in trouble—but yes, we used it. Send one of your men to Tombstone to get an ambulance. There are four wounded men up there, the rest are dead."

"Charlie, you hear him?" Jim asked an older man on horseback.

"I'll go get the dead wagon, Jim. Be careful, boys. That damn Clanton may try something else."

"Thanks for coming," Slocum told the man.

The rest turned their horses and they took the west fork in the road, heading for Nogales. Alkali dust boiled up from their horses' hooves. The sun beat down hot on the greasewood flats they crossed. The riders were quiet. Several of the men asked Slocum about the Gatling gun, and he told them not to say much about it so as to save the ranch manager from getting in any trouble. But he knew word would get out that someone had either stolen one from the fort or used the ranch's weapon.

Slocum rode most of the way stirrup to stirrup with Rosa. They watered their horses on the shallow creek and ate from a couple of Mexican women vendors at Patagonia, then they went on southwest. It was long past midnight when they crossed the border and rode the short distance to Ira Moulton's hacienda.

Armed guards stopped them, looked them over, then told Slocum they could go ahead.

Moulton got up when they arrived and shook hands with them. "Welcome to my hacienda. The women will fix your men some food and show you where to sleep. Ah, O'Riley, at last we meet. And this lovely lady is, of course, Rosa. How good you look with all these dusty men."

Moulton's woman showed her to a bath and told Slocum he could join her later.

After checking the mare and being pleased with her condition after all she'd been through, Moulton invited the men into the house to drink some wine as well as to talk about the entire recovery operation.

"I can't believe that you got both horses back from the Clantons." Moulton shook his head in amazement under the large overhead lamp in the great room.

"They aren't that smart," Slocum said.

"After tonight, I am going back to the East where I belong," O'Riley said, downing his second glass of wine.

"I'll pay you in the morning," Moulton said. "I must say, you are a man of your word."

"I'd never have made it if not for Slocum, Jim, and Rosa." O'Riley shook his head in disbelief.

Moulton agreed. "You were lucky. Didn't you have a wife?"

"Oh, that bitch. She ran out on me in Tucson."

"Really? Where did she go?"

"With some groom who used to work for me. She went to Preskit, last I heard."

"I'm sorry to hear that." He started to pour O'Riley some more wine, but the Irishman stopped him.

"No, I've had enough. I'll be leaving for Tucson in the morning and then head back East as quick as I can. I hope that bitch dies in a whorehouse." O'Riley rose to his feet. "Where is my room?"

"First one down the hall on the right. Sleep tight."

"I will."

"If you need anything, there's a girl in the kitchen who will get it for you."

"Thanks." O'Riley spoke to Slocum. "Slocum, I'll settle with you in the morning."

"Sure. Thanks to both of you." Slocum shook Moulton's hand and went off after O'Riley.

Slocum stopped where O'Riley stood in his room's doorway. "I really didn't believe I'd ever be here with my horses to collect that money," said O'Riley. "I am truly in your debt."

"I have little to say about that, except you need more faith in yourself. You have to make up your mind and you can get things done."

"I saw that. Calero ended up sending that Gatling gun on your say-so. You get things done no one else could." O'Riley shook his head and lowered his voice. "Do you think you could get my wife back for me?"

Slocum chuckled softly. "Do you really want her back? You've been bad-mouthing her since I met you back in Diamond City, and just a few minutes ago it sounded like you didn't want her."

"I know. I'm still not sure, but I think maybe I do."

"I'll consider it if you decide you really do want her back."

With a nod, Slocum went on down the hall, shaking his head at the man's indecision. He entered the bedroom assigned to him and Rosa. Inside in the dark room, he shed his boots and clothes. He was stark naked when he put his knee on the bed, and in the dim light he could see Rosa's naked figure stirring in the bed. Her open arms demanding him, he slipped into them, brushing her silky skin and taking his place between her shapely legs and muscled calves.

Her expert hands pumped his pole, arousing more power that was soon buried in her hot vagina. His tongue floated in a massive saliva flow that forced him to swallow hard. His anticipation of what lay ahead made his brain spin like a roulette wheel as he sought her depths. The pleasure of using her so-receptive body sent his heart pounding like a stamping mill. He plunged away in the pleasure of enjoying her delights.

His thoughts swirled as Rosa moaned. O'Riley might want his wife back. And where were those bastards who had raped Rosa's cousin Nana? He drove deeper and deeper. *Oh my God. I have lots to do, Rosa. Lots to do besides plow your sweet butt. . . .*

13

Reality prodded Slocum from behind his scratchy, dry eyes when he awoke. O'Riley's horses had been delivered. Rosa had already fled the bed, leaving him alone to consider what to do next. The spot where she'd slept had no heat when he ran his palm across it, so she'd been up for a while.

Three of Clanton's Cowboys were on his own personal wanted list for their crimes. Gorman, Valdez, and Bach: those vicious rapists who had ravaged Rosa's cousin Nana in a senseless raid on her small village.

He needed to find them. They did not deserve to walk on the same earth as their victim—at least, not without paying for their crimes.

Slocum dressed and joined the others in the main room. Moulton was counting out the money to O'Riley. Jim nodded from behind his coffee cup. Rosa brought Slocum a cup of coffee as he watched O'Riley, who looked pleased at the money stacked in front of him on the table.

He paid Jim a hundred dollars for his help and thanked him. Then O'Riley paid Slocum his five hundred and gave Rosa a hundred for all her work. She bowed and thanked him, as though she hadn't expected that much.

"I am leaving for Tucson on the stage from Nogales this afternoon. I have been truly blessed by your help. If I can ever do you any good, please contact me at my home in Baltimore," O'Riley said. "I shall never again deliver a horse beyond the Mississippi unless I have your invaluable help."

Everyone laughed.

"Rosa, I have a fine home back there. I would be pleased to have you as my hostess."

She frowned at him in disbelief. "Me?"

"Yes, I admire you very much. Will you join me?"

"I—I don't think so." She chewed on her lip. Looking shaken, she seemed lost for an answer.

Slocum wasn't quite as surprised by the request. That morning, O'Riley had told Slocum he didn't think the hassle of trying to get his wife back was worth it and that it sure would be nice if he had a loyal woman like Rosa instead. To Slocum it sounded a bit like a question. He told O'Riley that he was about to part ways with Rosa, and that if O'Riley really thought he'd be happy with her, he should ask Rosa to go with him.

"While you're thinking about his offer, I've got a ranch," Jim said. "You could be my hostess. Mine may not be as fancy as his, but I bet you'd feel more comfortable there."

Numbly, she nodded, then looked quickly at Slocum. "Are you leaving—too?"

"I need to move on."

About to cry, she shook her head. "I was not ready to decide today."

She twisted away and went to O'Riley and kissed his cheek. "I know you are rich and sincere, but I belong here in the desert. I could never live in a fancy house in a land of proper-mannered people. But thank you—"

"I would treat you like a queen."

"I can imagine that. But I am not leaving the land."

"All right. If I can ever help any of you, contact me," O'Riley said and left the room.

She stopped before Jim and looked down at his dusty boots. "You know my past and you'd offer me a place in your house?"

"I have, and I will hold nothing against you."

"Thank you. I will decide today. Let me have some time to consider all this."

"Sure."

She went to Slocum and took his hand. "We must talk."

He nodded and told the other two he would be back.

In the bedroom, she dropped her butt on the bed. Her dark eyes filled with tears, and she tried to shake away the obvious sadness. "I had thought that when you were gone, I would go back to where you found me. I had no real plans. I never expected O'Riley to offer me a position."

"He asked me and I told him to ask you."

"What about Jim?"

"He never asked me a thing, but he must want you. Jim is not a big talker. I don't think he'd ever mistreat you."

"I know—he's a very polite, nice man. Where will you go?" she asked.

"I don't know. But I have enemies, and staying in one place too long is not healthy for me. I've been in this part of the country too long already. It's best I move on. I can't promise you a thing—my life is too hacked up by things gone by."

"I could live on the run."

"It is hard to shed two sets of tracks. If they caught you, my enemies could use you as bait. I simply don't want that risk in your life."

"I won't forget you." She dropped her chin in defeat. "You will be in my greatest memories. Oh, this is horrible. How old is Jim?"

"Forties, I guess, but he appears healthy enough."

She folded her hands in her lap and didn't look up at him. "I will give him a honeymoon and see. I can always go back to Diamond City."

"I hope it works for both of you."

"Yes—so do I."

"Good, I'll ride on then. No need for me to be in the middle of all this."

"I would love one more session with you."

He shook his head. "We've had our fun."

"Just selfish of me. But if you'd not stolen my heart enough to make me chase you down on a burro, I'd never have had all this fun." She smiled from behind her wet lashes. "Leave me to clean up. Someday we will meet again. If not, I will always have a good memory of you, hombre."

"Yes," he said and rose, leaning forward and kiss her. *Good-bye, Rosa.*

An hour later, Slocum left Moulton's hacienda and rode for Nogales. He had a good picture of Jim and Rosa standing together before the great casa, waving good-bye as he rode off aboard a light-footed, dark chestnut horse, another gift from his host. A much better-looking horse, and a higher-spirited animal, than Spook. His replacement mount possessed instant speed and a big heart; Slocum called him King since he reminded him of the racehorse stallion.

His next stop was Tombstone. He wanted answers about where those three Cowboys who raped Nana were. He intended to cut them out of the Clanton bunch and make them pay for their crimes.

In the queen city of mines, he heard from Marshal Morgan Earp, the one Earp Slocum considered his friend, about a woman named Carla who ran a house of girls. He found Carla, who invited him into her parlor. He could see past the open side door into the adjoining bedroom with a large bed. Tall and rather slim waisted, Carla wore a lacy dress and served him a fair brand of whiskey. Her cleavage was not large, but she knew how to expose it for a man to admire. They sat at a small table in her private room and she toasted his good health while sitting opposite him.

"What are your needs today, sir?" She clinked her fine glass to his.

"I am looking for some men. One man with a scar above his right eye and lots of knife scars on his belly."

"Any other features?"

"Some time ago he'd been shot in the left shoulder."

She shook her head. "You will have to find a *puta* to tell you about him. I have never done business with such a man."

"A young Mexican with two fingers on his right hand shot off."

"Hernando Valdez. A cowardly son of a bitch. He works for Old Man Clanton."

"He frequents your services?"

"Only once. I barred that bastard from coming back."

Slocum lifted his glass of whiskey. "You know where he stays?"

"A place below the border on the Santa Cruz River. He has a common-law wife down there, they say."

Slocum poured more liquor in her glass and set the bottle down. Meeting her pale blue eyes, he nodded at her. "A black-bearded German."

"Five feet, eight inches tall? He could be Adolph Bach."

He agreed. "Sounds like him, and that's the name I was given."

"He actually bit the nipple off a dove one night. She liked to have bled to death. They nearly hung him. If some of the Cowboys hadn't taken his side, then others would have lynched him on the saloon porch. They barely saved his life."

"Where's he at?"

"He has a wife and some kids on the San Pedro below St. David. Who else?"

Slocum sat back. "That's all."

Carla perked up. "Now can we talk business? You look like a very virile man. My business is to offer my girls' services to you, sir."

"They tell me you're a very respected lady in the trade. How did you get in such a business? You hardly look the image of a madam."

"Thank you, you have a silk tongue, but better than that, you look like a very virile male. I was once a decorated major's wife. I was coddled and protected by his rank, but one day he went off to give his life to his country. Afterward, I was courted by several officers in my widowhood and I learned much about men's anatomies that was different than that of my very well-endowed late husband. In my ignorance, I thought all men were provided with an ample-size appendage, like my husband. But I found many who had considerable problems in their private life with this matter. Like one man whose apparatus was entirely too short, some who had problems rising to the occasion, and others who fired their gun too soon. I am sure you understand?"

He nodded so she continued. "I found that I was not a one-man woman either. So I make a lively living and enjoy my discretions. And what is your interest in these individuals you quizzed me about?"

"They severely raped a young woman who lives in a mountain Mexican village."

"I don't doubt that. Why is it your job to punish them?"

"'Cause no one else cares."

"I say, you not only are appealing, but you are generous to take on such revenge for her."

He nodded. "And before they do something worse to another innocent girl."

She nodded firmly. "They don't deserve any mercy."

"None."

"How can I help?"

"If you learn anything about them, leave word at Hamby Cox's café."

"I will do that, sir. Now, if your plans for the day are not pressing, perhaps you could take an hour's time to spend with an admirer."

"Those are your wishes?"

"Indeed they are, sir." She rose and untied the belt on her fancy robe.

He nodded and put his hat over on its crown atop the dresser. Then he unbuckled his holster and redid it to hang the gun on the top post of her chair. He toed off his boots and then undid his belt buckle and dropped his pants. When he lifted them to put them up, a small amount of dust scattered from them and she laughed.

"He came in a cloud of dust," she said dramatically, then stepped in to squeeze his manhood. "My, my, how delightful," she announced.

He shed his shirt for her next, then he stepped over and peeled the robe off her shoulders. Her body looked very inviting. With purpose, he bent her over and kissed her hard.

Her blue eyes fluttered and he swept her up to deposit her on the bed. Besides her sculptured features, her snow-white skin gleamed in the room's soft light. He placed her body, that of a thirty-year-old, on the bed. He moved over the top of her and she spread her legs in a V in the air with a soft laugh.

"All I need to do with you, sir, is to say ready, set, and go."

His half-full dick plunged into her opening, and she cried out from pleasure. "Take me. Just take me."

At her command, he lunged into her and she sighed, obviously pleased. But her vagina, he discovered, was muscled and waves of contractions soon squeezed his shaft. No wonder she never settled down in matrimony like most good military widows would have done. This machine of hers was as hungry as a tiger and also very pleasurable. She bucked like a wild horse on the complaining mattress and her nails scratched his back as she became lost in her own fury of passion. The squeezing pressure of her cunt was as arousing as her efforts to swallow his tool in her flat, muscular belly.

Out of wind and desperate to end this climb, he felt his testicles squeeze hard, and his cannon fired deep inside of her. Her collapse sent the slick wetness out of her in a flood over his sac.

He kissed her hard on the mouth, then braced himself over her. "You are a powerful woman."

With a smug smile on her lips, she rocked him with her hands on his hips. "Surely you have another round left in you for a poor woman who seldom gets such fine treatment from a real man."

He shoved his dick back inside her and she blinked her eyes as if shocked. "Coming up," he said.

Carla raised her head off the pillow and pursed her lips for him. He covered them hard with his own and she came out of their wet kiss shaking her head in disbelief and pushing the hair back from her face before she settled on her back. "Wow, I'm impressed. Come by more often."

He smiled at her and began pushing his new erection inside her. The session proved almost depleting enough to keep him there longer. But he wanted to locate the rapists' locations, realizing they might not be home when he found them. Old Man Clanton might have them occupied in his skulduggery.

In the afternoon heat, Slocum rode over to St. David. He knew a woman by the name of Alma who lived there. She was divorced from her husband, who had multiple wives. She owned twenty irrigated acres, milked a handful of Jersey cows, sold butter and eggs, and raised her three teenage children in the LDS faith. He rode in the back way, coming in from the desert, to keep down the gossip. He got off his horse, opened the back barbwire Texas gate, and led King inside the alfalfa patch, where the sweet smell of the legume filled the air.

Walking along the edge of the field, his horse stole a few mouthfuls of the shoe-top-high crop. A brindle, wide-bellied cow bawled for her calf, who answered from the whitewashed small barn. A stock dog barked, and when Slocum rounded the pens, a tall lady came out on the porch, pinning her graying hair back.

"Well," Alma drawled with a knowing grin. "I figured you'd lost your map to my place, big man."

He shook his head and tied King at the horse rack. "I knew you were busy and I haven't been in this area for a very long time."

She shooed him in through her back door and, once inside the kitchen, she threw her arms around him and they kissed. "Man oh man, am I ever glad to see you."

He held her loosely around the waist and rocked her from side to side. She was almost as tall as he was, and it felt good for him to hold her again. Something about this tall woman always found a big place in his heart.

"You look good," he said.

"This gray hair says I'm not getting any younger."

"And you have not remarried?"

She frowned. "I was not cut out to share a husband with a sweet young thing he kept in his bed at home while he expected me to make him money."

"I thought maybe someone saw all the good things in your heart and married you."

They kissed again. A serious look spread over her handsome tanned face. "Most men around here think with their peckers. More children and more income is what they want. I've heard enough of their preaching: 'You should be married, Alma, and be busy bringing more children into this world.' That ain't what God sent me here for."

"Where are your kids?" He looked around the room.

"Gone to Tucson for a church gathering with their father's family. So I'm a free woman. What do you need from—me?"

"Ah, more of this would be nice, but I need to go find some mean men who hurt a young woman."

She put her cheek on his shoulder. "Shucks, I thought you came to see me."

"I did, but I also want to locate a man they say has a farm below here—a German, Adolph Bach. He rides for Old Man Clanton."

"I've heard of him," she said. "He's a got young Mexican woman there. They say he beats her regular-like. No one likes him."

"When do you think I could catch him at home?"

She turned up her long hands, calloused from doing a man's work. "I don't know. Are you hungry?"

He shrugged. "Not too hungry—unless you have some peach pie."

"Now, how did you guess I had some of that?"

"I can smell the evidence on you."

"What else can you smell?"

"A very fine woman."

She put a finger by his nose and grinned big. "You remember that. It's very important to me. Pie's coming up."

He sat at the table, slowly masticating the bites of sweet peach pie. Saliva flooded his mouth and the aroma wafted up his nostrils. *My, what a heavenly place to sit in the cool shade of her kitchen with a breeze coming through the house and eat such heavenly food.*

The frosting on the cake was the attentive look on her face while she clearly wondered when he would get through eating and race upstairs to enjoy her willing body. Not a bad way to live, considering he came there to kill a man—who needed it.

She reached over and squeezed his hand. Her blue eyes danced. "You ready?"

"Sure."

14

The bloody sundown coming in the west window outlined Alma's tall, naked form as she stood in the last light at the foot of the bed. The bloody flare of that light outlined her shapely form as she leaned over to ask Slocum if he wanted some fried ham with mashed potatoes and gravy for supper.

"Fine. Is the sheepherder shower hooked up?" he asked, throwing his legs off the bed.

"Yes. It should be warm enough. With the kids gone, it gets a chance to heat up some. Need soap and a towel?"

"I do." He stood up and pulled on his pants.

She hugged and kissed him, then put on her housecoat, buttoning it up the front. Seated on the bed, he put on his socks and boots, still thinking about their lovemaking. What a delicious way to spend a few hours. His balls felt completely depleted, but oh, what a great day. A second lovely woman to entertain him. *Whew!* His back nagged at him when he stood up. Better go take a bath while he had the chance.

"Put your pretty horse in the barn too," she said when he passed her in the kitchen and kissed her on the cheek.

"Thanks. He'll appreciate that."

"I do too." She shook her head at him and then blushed.

"Count me in on that as well."

*   *   *

The windmill out back creaked along on the evening breeze, cranking out water to fill a large holding tank to see to the livestock's needs. During a short recess she took from him that afternoon while he took a nap, Alma had milked the cows and fed her chickens and pigs. Then she'd taken a quick shower and climbed back in bed as if refreshed.

At the shed's porch he undressed and then stepped under the showerhead. The water that came down on his head when he pulled the rope wasn't icy, but it damn sure wasn't warm. Wet, he quickly soaped up, then rinsed away the residue. Drying off, he went back toward the house. King was in a stall crunching on alfalfa hay. It would be hard to leave Alma. It was that way with all the good women he knew in this world.

The next morning when the sun came up he sat on the ridge behind some boulders and turned the field glasses on Bach's jacal.

He'd learned from Alma that Bach was a vicious man and several people had felt the bite of his temper. Bach once used a bullwhip to beat up a man who laid adobe bricks for him because of some cracked bricks that Bach said he had caused. People told Alma that all adobe bricks crack and it was to be expected for some to be lost. The brick man almost lost his eye in that encounter. Few people in the region even wanted to talk about Bach.

At Bach's jacal, a young Mexican woman with a baby in a sling milked three goats on her doorstep. Then she fed some chickens. No sign of a horse in the corral—her man obviously was not there. Slocum slipped back over the ridge, caught his hobbled horse, and took the back way into Alma's place.

She was busy canning when he got back. The kitchen was all steamed up. The new miracle-lidded glass jars were a big benefit for home food preservation. Of course, the church had a canning processing operation, but Alma wanted her own independence from the ward's warehouse, so she did her own.

Slocum offered to help, but she dismissed his offer. "Was he home?"

"No, and no telling when he'll be back either."

"Go get some sleep upstairs. You left here way too early. I won't forget you."

He knew she wouldn't. So he kissed her and hiked upstairs. The breeze was coming through the bedroom's open windows, making the windmill outside creak hard. He undressed and fell asleep quickly.

Thunder rolled him off the bed. He laughed once he was standing on the floor getting his bearings. Just a monsoonal shower. He went to the window and bent over to look out the lower opening. Large raindrops were driving in. Putting down the windows to save the room from the water, he heard her coming upstairs.

"Wow, rain in the desert," she said, sounding excited.

"Things happen." He hugged her.

"Glad you shut out the rain." They kissed as more grumbles rolled over the roof. They kept on seeking each other until they spilled onto the bed and shuffled their clothing around to get together.

The rain lasted a long time and so did they, until at last their wild lovemaking was curtained when he came again and they sprawled on the bed, exhausted.

She was on her belly and elbows beside him. "You ever think about holing up somewhere?"

He shook his head and smiled. "It would never work."

"We could go up in Utah and find an isolated place."

"Never work. I've got too many enemies. They'd find me."

"Could we try it sometime?"

He leaned over and kissed her. "I wouldn't put you and your kids through all that hell."

"Hey, we'd make do."

"Rain's moved on."

She made a wry face at him and pushed herself up, and her pear-shaped breasts shook as she moved away, looking weary as she reflected on her situation. Great body and wonderful woman—Slocum would really miss her. Nothing else he could do. No way they could hide out for long from the men who sought him.

That evening he rode down for a quick check of Bach's jacal.

When he saw no horse in the corral, he went back to Alma's place through the same back gate. Water seeped in his boot soles as he walked King around the field. *Free irrigation*, he thought, and smiled.

Alma was busy fixing supper when he came into the house after putting his horse in the stall. He kissed her, then put up his hat and gun belt.

"We got over two inches of rain."

"The river is flooding some," he said.

"Shame we can't hold that for a dry spell. Our artesian wells won't last forever."

He knew their irrigation water came from capped deep wells. Some used the water from the San Pedro River for their operations, but it was an undependable source.

Her supper included fried chicken, spinach, fresh green beans, and some homemade sourdough bread and peach pie. She knew how to entice a man to stay. They went to bed early and he got up in the middle of the night to be near Bach's jacal at sunup to check on the man's presence.

He listened to the topknot quail whit-wooing out in the bunch grass and chaparral. A small purple light began to frame the Chiricahuas. Through the glasses he could see the outline of a big horse in the pen. His man was there.

Slocum put the glasses up in his saddlebags and began to work his way around the place, coming up from behind through the mesquite. The milk goats bleated at him. He shooed them away, with his right hand on his pistol grip. Outside the jacal, he squatted beside the ruins of another adobe building to wait for Bach to appear.

Time went by slowly. The sun came up over Slocum's shoulder; it would be in the outlaw's eyes when he came out. Slocum watched him come out the doorway, groping in his pants for his dick—to piss, no doubt.

When Adolph Bach looked up, he started at the sight of Slocum. His hand quit trying to find his pecker and he went for a gun that must have been in his back pocket. When he swung the small handgun around, Slocum shot him in the chest and sent him to his knees. Bach snarled and tried to raise his gun arm. Big mistake—Slocum shot him again in the middle of his chest.

A woman inside began screaming. So did some babies. Slocum holstered the six-gun and turned his back on the death scene. That worthless sumbitch would rape no more innocent women.

He found King, unhobbled him, and mounted up. He was back at Alma's place by midmorning.

She looked up from churning butter when he came inside and took off his hat. She knew by the look on his face what had happened. He saw the question in her eyes and nodded.

"It's done."

"Good." She went to turning the crank harder. "I'll be through in a minute or so."

He sat down on a chair. "There's no rush."

"When will you have to leave here?"

"In the morning."

She looked hard at him. "Stay the whole day tomorrow and leave the next morning. Then my kids will be back, and I'll get back on the track I follow every day."

He couldn't deny her the small request and nodded again. "A deal."

All smiles, she said, "Wonderful. I want to put this butter in the cooler. I'll meet you upstairs." She made a face over something. "I need a shower. Then I'll be up there. Nap awhile."

He laughed, went upstairs, and undressed. Soon he was asleep. He woke easy-like when he felt her strong fingers massaging his sleeping dick. Her breath in his ear and her tongue teasing him caused him to smile. Damn, she was tall with an amazing hard body from all the farmwork she handled. He rolled over against her, and she got up to straddle his flanks and the half-full erection. In a few seconds, she stuck his prick in her vagina and began to ride him with a grin on her face.

He strained hard to push deeper inside her each time, but she was the guide and was enjoying every minute from her efforts. The bed ropes screamed under them, and they were both lost in the wild involvement of their act.

Then she dove onto the bed beside him and he sprung on

top of her. First she held her legs straight up in the air, but then she folded them up for him to really get after her ass. His balls were bouncing off her butt as he sought the deepest place in her vagina to let fly his load. With his dick buried in her to the hilt, she cried out in pleasure at his explosion. They lay in a pile and tried to recover their breath and to clear their brains of the fog set off by the climax.

They soon snuggled in each other's arms, kissing and seeking a closeness to seal them into one. Damn, she was a wonderful woman, and that hideout in Utah she'd mentioned might be heaven. But he needed to be honest with himself—they'd find him even up there. He better make the best of their reunion during the next twenty-four hours, 'cause he had to leave soon.

Two more men must pay for their savage raping of Nana, and then Slocum could move on.

His shoulders shook from the excitement coursing through him from holding Alma's sensuous, naked body tight against his. He closed his eyes and thanked the powers that be for sharing her with him even for a small space in time.

15

On his trip south below the border, he began to question store-keepers and the like along the way to where this Valdez lived. No one could say if he was at his small farm, but Slocum intended to stop near his place and check it out. No telling if Valdez knew by this time that his associate Adolph Bach was dead. The extra day and night he had spent at Alma's might have let the bastards realize that someone was settling a debt on them for something they'd done.

Two horses were in the corral at Valdez's jacal when Slocum scoped them with the field glasses from a distance. In the last light of sundown, he rode back to a cantina where he was served a hot meal. A short, brassy woman in her thirties with big tits and a large belly brought him his food.

"You want to fuck me?" she asked, standing with her hands on her hips and her feet apart as if she were challenging him.

He looked up at her mildly in the smoky cantina. "No."

"What's wrong with me for you?" she demanded.

With a shake of his head to dismiss her, he started to pick at his food.

She slapped the table with her palm. "I asked you—"

When she reached for him, he caught her wrist in a vise grip and drew her close to his face. "I want to eat. Now get out of my sight."

"You gawdamn gringo—" Two of the bartenders came on the run and furiously dragged her away, kicking and screaming. They apologized to him and hauled her into the back room, and soon she was quiet. Slocum wondered what they were doing with her, but in a short while customers began to file into the back room, one at a time. When they came out, they waved for another to go in there while buttoning their pants.

He didn't particularly care what had happened to her, but after he paid for his meal and beers, he passed the open door on his way out and could see that they had gagged her, tied her spread-eagled on top of a bed, and invited everyone to dip his wick in her. Good enough.

Later, alone in the desert, he wrapped himself in a blanket against the night's cold. He wasn't more than an hour away from Valdez's place. He planned to surprise that worthless man in the morning before dawn if he came out of his jacal.

Slocum woke and checked the moon. The time was about two hours until dawn, by his calculations. Under the starlight, he saddled King and rode off in the cool night to find Valdez and settle his business with the outlaw.

He arrived at his destination without incident. Grateful for the moonlight, he hobbled King and made his way through the tall mesquite brush to the back of the place. At last he found a spot where he could view the open doorway.

Squatted down on his heels, he passed the time wondering where he'd find Gorman. Maybe he was in Mexico too. A man with a scar above his right eye should not be hard to find. People wouldn't forget someone like that. Just as the sun was rising, he heard horses coming and dropped farther back to avoid detection, wanting to hear what was going on next.

"Hombre! Valdez, wake up! They shot Bach two nights ago. You may be next. Get out of bed. Bach is dead!"

"Who shot him?"

"A pistolero. This is one tough bastard. Bach's wife said he shot her husband six times when he came out the door—he didn't have a chance. You better get up to the Old Man's, huh?"

"*Madre de Dios*. Do they have the name of his killer?"

"No, she didn't see him. He rode a shod horse, and we could not follow his tracks in the road dust.

"Why did he shoot Bach?"

"Who knows, but it might be for revenge. But you and him—you've done some things together, no?"

"We done many things together. Does this shooter work for Wells Fargo, do you think?"

"I don't know. Maybe they hired him. They're still looking for the buckboard and everything. But all that was burned and buried."

"You don't ever know nothing about *dees* Well Fargo men. I know several men *dey* kilt." Valdez coughed. "Angela, pack my things. I must go."

"I am going to warn Gorman."

"Good idea."

Where was Gorman? Slocum wanted that answer, and he figured this was his best chance to find him. Running low, he went for his horse, took off the hobbles, swung into the saddle, and headed out of the brush. He wanted a better look at this man who had come to warn Valdez. His knowledge about the buried robbery deal would thrill the Wells Fargo man to death. Perhaps he could follow the man to Gorman, find that bastard, take care of him, and come back for Valdez. If he could find Gorman, he could maybe wait there for Valdez to join him—surely they'd be together. And he would have more information on the robbery.

He halted his horse on the rise, and with his glasses trained on the road, waited for the man to ride by. He was galloping fast down the road, and the land was wide open—no cover at all for someone trying to stealthily follow a horseman, and no way to track him since he was about to join up with a well-traveled road. But Slocum did get a good look at him: He was medium build, a Mexican with slanted eyes—almost Chinese-looking, probably a half-blood even. Though Slocum could not put a name to him, Wells Fargo would know him. They had a list an arm long of the men who rode for Clanton.

Slocum knew he couldn't successfully follow this man to

Gorman. Even as Slocum lowered the glasses, preparing to head back and finish off Valdez, that outlaw himself appeared on the road, galloping hard after his informant. Muttering a curse, Slocum realized he couldn't catch up without foundering his own horse.

With Valdez staying who knows where, he'd be harder to find, but he would be found. He would also now be on Wells Fargo's list of persona non grata as someone who had been in on the buckboard holdup and murders of three of their employees. Good. So they thought it was an express company man who'd killed Bach.

Slocum headed for Tombstone to find the Wells Fargo man. In the Oriental Saloon he located Agent Holt and they went to the back of the room to talk.

"What do you know?" the agent asked, swilling his whiskey around in his glass.

"One of the men who was in on the Nogales buckboard robbery is dead."

Holt frowned. "Who's that?"

"Adolph Bach. And I found out some of the others who were involved."

Holt wet his lips. "Who?"

"A three-fingered Mexican named Valdez."

"I know him. Who else?"

"Carl Gorman, who's got a scar over his right eye. I overheard a Mex in his late twenties talking to Valdez three hours ago about the rig being burned up and buried. Did you find it?"

"We ain't, but now we'll have a better idea of what we're looking for. How did you get in on this?"

"Gorman, Bach, and Valdez viciously raped an innocent girl in the mountains down south. Bach is dead, and I want the other two's hides nailed to the shit house wall for what they did to her."

Holt raised the glass and toasted him. "So do I, but for other reasons. Three good men murdered. Where do you want the envelope for the money I owe you? This is the first real break I've had. You get one of them alive, please try to get as much as you can out of him before he rides off to hell."

"Hamby Cox over at the café will hold the money for me. Thanks," Slocum said.

Holt nodded and they parted.

What the hell. No telling what Holt would pay him. He'd take it and be glad. A small bonus for ridding the earth of more trash. For his part, he wished he'd gotten Valdez earlier in the day, but he'd just have to find him again—and Gorman was also still out there.

At the café, after digging in to a meal consisting of a bowl of stew and sourdough bread, he told Cox about expecting a letter.

The man nodded. "It will be here when you come for it."

Slocum paid him, tipped his waitress a dime, and headed for Joe Kelly's Livery to get King. Halfway there he stopped and checked the sun time—two or three o'clock. What was his newfound madam doing this time of day? She just might need some company.

A black maid answered the front door, then went upstairs to ask Miss Hunton if she had time to see him. Less than a minute after the maid disappeared, an excited Carla was standing at the top of the stairs. "Get right up here, you big hombre. I thought you'd left the country."

When he reached the top of the stairs, her arms went around his waist to hug him and she thanked the wide-eyed black girl. They went into Carla's suite and she closed the door. She lifted up on her toes and they kissed and then kissed some more.

"Why, I thought you'd sugar footed away from here. What made you come back? Wait, how long can you be here?"

"A night, if you want me that long." He wondered what she was going to do.

"Wonderful, take off your clothes behind that screen. I'll have them bring up some hot bathwater and we can have your clothes laundered."

"I don't—"

Her two fingers cut off his speech. "You are my guest, sir."

"Yes, ma'am." Then he took off his gun belt and began to undress with her assistance.

"Your bathwater will be here shortly. Get behind the silk screen. The help doesn't need to see that super cock of yours."

He furrowed his eyebrows. "Now, how in the hell did you order that? You've been here all the time."

She herded him behind the screen and, at the knock on the door, loudly said, "Bring the water in, girls."

Giggling over her secret, she stood on her toes and whispered to him, "I pulled the red velvet cord three times. That means bring me bathwater."

He caught her under the cheeks of her tight ass and pulled her tight against him. "Sneaky damn trick."

They both laughed.

"Bring up some rinse water in ten minutes, girls."

"Yes, ma'am." And they left the room.

Slocum's bath went smoothly, with Carla brushing his back with a long-handled brush. The help brought two buckets of warm water, and she showed them out after giving them his clothes in a bundle to be washed. Then she strode back, looked down at him, and shook her head in mild disbelief. "How did I get so lucky to have you return?"

"You knew I was looking for those men. One of them has gone on to hell. Another one ran to hide, probably at Clanton's hideout in Mexico, and the third man is missing."

Standing on a footstool, she rinsed him with the first bucket as he stood at his full height in the tub. He reached down for the other one and then handed the pail to her. After the water was sloshed over him, he held out his hand for the towel. Instead, she moved in to dry him herself.

"So what will you do next?"

"Go into Mexico and look for Gorman. He may be down there."

"Maybe you should stay here a few days and they will think you are gone."

"Might work, but they aren't dumb."

She looked up from where she knelt, drying his lower body, and rose. "I am simply pleased that you returned—to me."

"Find me some Mexican dress, leather pants, high-top boots,

a serape, and a sombrero. I can pay you. I'll buy a Mexican Big Horn saddle and ride down there."

"Oh, *sí*."

He gave her a friendly shove. "I can mumble enough Spanish to get by."

"We won't shave you then."

"It's your skin."

She shook her head and dismissed his concern. "I will send Lola out to buy these items. She's the most dependable for this job, and she can measure your clothing with strings."

"Lots of trouble for you."

"I will make a pattern from your feet. This may take a day or two to get all of it." She looked at him for his approval.

"Fine."

After his feet's pattern was traced on wrapping paper, Carla instructed Lola in what to do. Carla came back to her naked guest, who sat on the bed after she closed the door.

"Well, now I have you trapped in here." She began unbuttoning her dress before him.

He rose and helped her undress. She soon joined him in his nakedness and they kissed some more. Then they spilled on the bed, in no big hurry to do any more than savor each other. With him on his back and her braced on top of his chest, she asked, "How many of these men are left?"

"Two remain."

"That should be no problem for you."

"Put some word out that if either of them show up here in town, people should get word to you."

"I can do that." She winked mischievously at him. "Now let's work on ourselves."

They kissed and fell into a furious lovemaking spree. In a short while he was coupled with her and enjoying the luxury of her body. Out of breath and pounding her hard, he came at last and they dissolved like wilted flowers and napped.

His own clothes were back, placed on the table outside the door to her suite. She recovered them and he dressed. Then she ordered supper for them and some wine.

After a fine meal of prime rib and potatoes, he excused himself, promising to return later.

"Don't knock when you return. Simply come on in," she said as she rose to kiss him.

It was midweek and Big Nose Kate's was quiet. The bartender told him none of the Cowboys were in town, nor had he seen any of them since Saturday night. Slocum finished his beer and went on.

He knew there was a Mexican bar in town and he went there next. The whore who sat in the chair next to him, showing off her small cleavage, told him that Gorman had not been in Tombstone for several weeks. Although she had no idea where the outlaw was at the moment, her eyes lit up at the sight of a silver dollar and she smiled. "I do know he has been staying at a place south of here, a ranch that his brother owns, and is helping him round up his cattle."

He put the coin down flat. *"Muchas gracias."* Then he left her and went next door into a barbershop that was still open. Such places stayed open almost around the clock because so many miners worked such long hours and then drank before they thought about their appearances.

"You want a shave?" the man asked, looking to make another fifty cents. "You look like you need one."

Slocum shook his head. The damn facial hair would not grow out as fast as he wanted it anyway. He paid the man thirty-five cents for the haircut, but when he stepped outside, he retreated quickly right back inside. Four Cowboys he recognized had ridden up the street. Back in the shadows of the barbershop he wondered if either of the men he wanted, Gorman or Valdez, was with them.

When they were past, he trailed them, staying out of sight. They left their horses and guns at the O.K. Corral. Then the four went to the staircase of a brothel, whooping and hollering about how horny they were. He doubted they could screw a goat as drunk as they were. His next move was to separate them somehow, then work on them one at a time until he had answers to where they'd buried the guards and driver, plus the remains of the missing buckboard.

A smile crossed Slocum's face as one of their lot sat on the bottom step and waved them on. He was either too broke or too drunk to go for a whore—sitting there, he looked like he suffered from both states. There was no patrol on the board-walk, and Slocum crossed the street and hustled the Cowboy off into the dark alley. Then he shoved him into an unused stable. The room smelled of old hay and old, soured horseshit. Barely enough light came in through the cobwebby window for Slocum to see the man's face.

"You work for Old Man Clanton?"

"Fuck, yes."

"You ever have an ear cut off?"

"Hell, no. What are you going to do to me?" The man tried to lean away and put his hands up to protect his face.

"Where's that buckboard buried?"

"I—I don't know."

"What's your name?"

"Yancy, Yancy Dobbins."

"If I cut off half your ear, will you tell me where they planted it?"

"I don't know where." The kid's voice moved an octave higher.

"You know." Slocum shook him by the handful of shirt gathered in his fist. "Tell me."

"No—no, I wasn't even there."

"Tell me!" His voice raged in his throat. "Tell me!"

"All right. All right. I'll tell you who did it."

"Start, but you better be telling me the truth."

"Gorman was the head guy. He said the damn guards started shooting at them, so they had to kill them. They figured the law would really get after them for it. So they burned the buck-board and buried it and the men on the Fort Huachuca lands in a sandy dry wash. They thought no one would figure it out."

"You better go get on your horse and get the hell out of this country. Old Man Clanton finds out you told me this, he will cut off your balls." The man visibly trembled as Slocum con-tinued, "Dobbins, you need to get out of Arizona as fast as your horse will carry you."

"Yeah, yeah." He swallowed hard and as soon as Slocum released him, he scurried like a half-crazed rabbit out of the shed, down the alley, and all the way to the O.K. Corral. In minutes, Slocum stood on the street corner and watched him race toward the dark outline of the Whetstones in the west. He damn sure was not going back to the Clanton fortress.

In the morning, Slocum rode over to Fort Huachuca and spoke to the commander, Colonel Butler, about the situation. The officer called in the Apache scouts and their commander.

"The guards and the burned-up buckboard from the Wells Fargo robbery are buried in a dry wash somewhere on the fort. Find it. Mr. Slocum, make yourself comfortable. Lieutenant Lions will show you around. They'll find it in a few hours if it's here."

"Thank you, sir."

An hour later in the mess hall, a private reported to Lions.

"Sir, the site has been located. They've found some bodies varmints had dug up."

"There, Mr. Slocum. They found it. What shall I tell the colonel?"

"Thank him. I will tell the Wells Fargo agent where the site is, and no doubt the U.S. marshal will investigate the matter since it's on federal land."

"Yes, it will be looked at by them."

"Thank the colonel for all of his efforts," Slocum said and went to get his horse.

Slocum rode back to Tombstone, put up his horse, and took a bath while Carla settled an internal labor problem among her whores, an argument between two whores about who did what to whom. Out of the tub and drying himself, Slocum chuckled. She was damn good at her job. Never swore and always acted very calm about things—until he turned the gas burner on inside of her and she made a helluva lover. He'd never ever seen anyone quite like her in bed.

She rapped on the door, then came in and smiled at seeing his nakedness. "You had a good day?"

"Yes. The buckboard's been found on the fort land. I got an envelope from the company too at Cox's today. They sent me two hundred fifty dollars for the information I gave Holt. I wonder what they will pay for finding the buckboard."

She hugged him tenderly and snuggled her cheek to his beard. "Shall we eat first?"

"Oh, before we fire up?"

She laughed and gave him a small shove, then took him back to kiss him. "Let's do that first. I fear that when you leave me I will be so depressed without your forces that I may be lost."

"Lord, lord." He squeezed her tight to him.

"Have you been in the bedroom?" she asked.

"No. Why?"

"Your Mexican wardrobe came today."

He pushed open the door and saw the clothing on the bed. "Well, señora, my disguise is here." Their laughter was pleasure filled.

They moved the clothes, exposing the sheets, and immediately climbed into bed naked to join together. She closed her eyes once she was lying underneath him.

"Oh, my lands, Slocum. You are so smooth and you can turn me on like a coal oil lamp on fire. Already my heart is pounding—I've been hours behind trying to catch up with a lover so many times . . . maybe it is your presence. Oh my God—"

They were pressing hard to be one. The muscles in her vagina closed in on his shaft. His mouth, earlier powder-dry from his long ride in the heat over to the fort and back, was all at once flooded with moisture. His brain swirled like a dozen dust devils he'd seen dance across the greasewood and grass valleys he'd traveled over. With everything centered on their attachment, he worked harder and harder to send her over the mountaintop.

And then his shot went off. He felt her gather up at that second and fall into a chasm. A deep one—good.

16

In the morning Slocum left for Mexico. He stopped at the Peralta Springs Ranch, and the *segundo*, Juan Calero, put him up for the night. After the evening meal, they laughed around the campfire about the firefight with the Cowboys on the west slopes of the Mule Mountains with the Gatling gun.

"We heard five men were killed, and four injured," one of the vaqueros said.

Another spoke up. "And eight good horses dead."

"They probably stole that many more from some poor ranchero in Sonora."

"Hey, Slocum, you have a prettier horse this time, but where is that good-looking woman?"

"I think she's with a rancher I know. He had prettier horses and a finer casa than I did."

They laughed about that. Slocum turned in early—and a woman's finger on his lips silenced and woke him in the middle of the night. She lifted the blanket and climbed in the hammock with him.

"She was crazy for leaving you?" she whispered.

He shook his head. "No."

Slocum thought he recognized her. The night was dark. She kissed him hard and felt for his dick. In minutes, she was under him and obviously enjoying his attentions to her. Her vagina felt tight and she was hot. He could tell she was suppressing her moans as much as she could. When he felt her breathing hard in his right ear, he turned up his speed and she gasped—then he came and she collapsed.

"Oh, *madre de Dios*, she was a stupid bitch," she whispered in his ear. "I knew when you said she left you, it was a big mistake for her." Her roll out of the hammock almost tossed him on the ground. She came back and, with her pear-shaped boobs bouncing over the side of the swing, kissed him hard on the mouth, then said, "You arc a real lover, *mi amigo*. Come back again, and if you have no woman with you, I'll find you. And take good care of that *grande* horse dick."

Then she was gone in the night, wrapped under her blanket. Covering her head in the dark made her hard for anyone to distinguish who she was. He knew who she was—the *segundo*'s fine wife. What next? He shook his head over the deal and went back to sleep.

The women served breakfast before daybreak. Strong coffee, eggs, and pork and chili peppers wrapped in fresh-made flour tortillas, and a cinnamon-apple mix wrapped in another tortilla. The women made sure he got two of those.

The big man's wife brought Slocum some bean burritos wrapped in brown paper. He thanked her and asked her name.

"Carmellia. *Vaya con Dios*, hombre."

As he rode away, he knew Carmellia, who lived at Peralta Springs Ranch, would be on his mind for many hot miles of travel that day. He would ride away on his light-footed horse and never mind a thing, save the fact that he would not have her sweet ass again in his bedroll that night.

The next evening he reached Agua Fría after sundown. He drank a warm beer in a smoky cantina where a teenage girl danced to a fast-strumming guitar with many flashes of her shapely brown legs under the red skirt. She could draw all the enthusiasm of the many drinkers, who were all near drunk.

Slocum shook his head and pushed away an ugly fat *puta* who came by and reached for his crotch. She curled her lip as she snarled at him and moved on. Outside, away from the circus of people drunk and horny, he found a vendor and ordered some food. Squatted at her small stove, she made him a wrapped-up burrito. He paid her a dime and went on. Alone and far enough away from the guitar's piercing sounds, he stepped into the shadows to consume his meal.

A small woman must have seen him. She joined him to stand close by. She spoke no words while he chewed his food slowly. She simply stood there and watched the passing traffic.

"Señor," she finally said in Spanish, not looking at him, "will you sleep alone tonight?"

"I am looking for an hombre with only two fingers and a thumb on his right hand."

"His name is Valdez. Hernando Valdez."

"Where can I find him?" He had to shake her arm to get her to pocket the silver coin he tried to hand her.

"At the rancho of Carlos Mendosa."

"Where is this place?"

"It is a desert rancho. They have lots of irrigation. It is south of here."

He paid her another dollar. "Is he down there now?"

She shrugged. "He rides north sometimes. He is a mean man to women. I try to avoid him."

"I understand that he is mean to women."

She nodded. "He is a *malo* hombre. You did not have to pay me for that."

"You would have expected me to pay for your services, so why not that?"

She shrugged.

"Now you can go home and sleep soundly by yourself."

"No. I always need more money. Good night, my lover."

He watched her put a shawl over her head, then move off into the shadows.

He rode the horse out into the desert and under a million stars. Hobbling him, he put his canvas ground cloth down on the spot he had cleared of rocks and stones with the sides of his new boots. A coyote's yap called out in the night. Its pack answered in lonely yelps. Under a single, thick cotton blanket shielding him from the cold, Slocum slept until just before dawn.

He rode back into town and found a vendor to cook him some eggs, meat, and a hot pepper burrito. Then he bought some grain for his horse from a sleepy teenage clerk who had just unlocked the store. There in the golden rosy glow of sunup he waited for the horse to eat his nose bag of grain while he drank the vendor's strong coffee from his own tin cup. Then he saddled up and rode off.

Later in the day he found a smaller village. There were several people in the square, and he'd seen more on the road heading there. Apparently, this was a holiday for saints. Many women had a covered bird under their arms with its multicolored long tail feathers exposed. There would be some chicken fights. These people loved such bloody feather fests.

Slocum knew there would be lots of music that night, some off-key, but most would be fine to dance to in the dust with someone of the opposite sex. They prayed here in the small mission and then drank there in the square. Most would inhale pulga, a thick, homemade beer made from fermented corn and sugar. Not his favorite drink. After a few glasses of the sweet-sour drink, many handsome women would forget they were married and adventure astray. After sundown, Slocum would have no problem finding a willing woman to dance with or to fuck. Most people expected to do both before the sun rose again.

The cantina served warm dark beer for ten cents. He bought a mug, then went outside on the shady porch with his back to the wall to watch the crowd. Still early in the day, before noon, a small, dirty-faced boy came up to him.

"Señor, may I stable your fine horse?"

"Where will he be?" he asked.

The boy pointed behind him without looking back. "At my *mamacita*'s casa and stables."

"I will go put this mug back inside and you can show me."

"*Gracias*. We will brush him down and he will be safe there."

Slocum held his hand up; he did not need the boy's entire sales speech. "Wait. I will be back pronto."

The boy bowed his head, "*Gracias*, señor."

Leading the horse, Slocum and the boy walked side by side through the crowd. Slocum did not miss the comments made by both men and women about this stranger in Mexican garb and his fine horse.

The mother's casa was a jacal behind the buildings on the square, and it had several corrals under the lip of the broad, dry wash beside it.

A short, good-looking woman in her early twenties with curly dark hair and nice, modest cleavage came out and nodded to him. "You wish for us to care for your horse, señor?"

"This hombre told me this was the best place in this town to stable him for the night."

"Ah, *sí*. My son's name is Ronaldo. This village is St. Thomas, and we have pens with hay and water for your animal."

"What is your name?" He studied the straight-backed young woman who was maybe five feet tall.

"Teresa Toya."

She looked like a toy to him. "And what is the holiday charge for those services?"

"We can stable your horse for twenty-five centavos, señor."

"Fine. And to feed him grain?"

"Ten cents more." Her dark eyes studied him.

"Will your husband allow you to dance with me tonight?"

She shook her head, which disappointed him, and then she said with a soft smile, "I am free to dance with you tonight, señor. I am a widow. My husband has been dead for several years."

Then he tipped his hat to her. "We shall dance tonight then."

Her smile sealed the deal and she led away his horse. Ronaldo ran off to find more business.

"I'll unsaddle him," he said as we moved after her. She shook her head that she did not need help.

"My name is Slocum."

She stopped and turned, using her hand to shade her eyes from the sun to look at him. "I won't forget you, Señor Slocum."

"Good." He went back to the square. A pleasant, attractive woman like her might have many suitors in such a large gathering. He felt pleased to know he had someone to dance with. More and more people were arriving. Maybe this event was close enough to attract Three Fingers Valdez.

By that time, people had begun to form a large circle on the flat of dry grass in back of the mission building, and word was out: The chicken fights were about to begin. People drove up in wagons and carts to stand in to see the fight over the inner circle's heads. Many vaqueros and even some ranch women sat on their horses to watch the feather fest.

A big-chested man in a gold-braided vest with a booming voice and wearing a great sombrero announced the first pairing, Gootsomething versus Antry. The birds were being held up overhead by the owner-trainers and the betting began. Sharp silver spurs were already strapped on the legs of both birds, and they gleamed in the bright sunlight.

The first fight was about to begin. The birds were placed on the ground and, when each had caught sight of its opponent, the man said, "Go!"

The two birds rushed at each other. Then, in a cloud of dust, they flew in the air and slashed at each other. The crowd roared. One had more red tail feathers than the other one. That one, which Slocum mentally dubbed "Red," scored the first strike, drawing blood with the first encounter. They stalked in a circle and flew at each other again. This time Red one took a beakful of his opponent's neck feathers and then pulled away with a lot of them. The other bird's neck looked strange with a featherless collar. Time and again they flew at each other and more plumage was lost. Then Red put out his opponent's eye. Half the crowd cheered, and the other half moaned, "oh," over the loss.

"Slocum," someone called out from beside him. He glanced down. It was Teresa standing beside him.

"Let me ride on your shoulders. I can't see." He removed his large sombrero, put it between his knees, and hoisted her up in the air. In a flash of her brown, shapely legs, she got her skirt wadded behind his head, hugged his forehead, and settled on top of him.

"Give me your hat," she said.

He gave it to her and they watched Red finish off his adversary.

"Am I too heavy?" she asked, sounding concerned.

He shook his head and squeezed her ankles. "I have you right where I want you."

She leaned over. "Yeah, how is that?"

"I will never tell."

Teresa riding on his shoulders entertained him. She whooped and hollered along with beating him with the big sombrero when she really became worked up about a bird winning.

"I'm not hurting you?" she asked during a small recess in the chicken-fighting action.

"No, I kinda like having a pretty lady riding on my shoulders."

"That doesn't sound so good." Then she laughed. "I like being tall for once in my life."

"Who's going to win the next fight?" he asked.

"Gregorio. He is always one of the best."

"Hey, gambler," Slocum shouted to the bet taker. "She wants to put two dollars on Gregorio's bird." When he reached in his pocket for the money, he released one of her ankles.

"You're on," the man said.

She held his forehead in both hands. "You scared me. I don't have two dollars to bet."

"Maybe we will have more."

After four more rounds, the rooster fighting ended and he had to let her down. Their gambling earned them ten pesos by compounding their bets. He told the man who took the wagers to pay Teresa. On the ground at last, straightening her skirt, she frowned at his words.

"I had no money in those bets," she protested.

"But you were the director sitting up there. It's only right you get the winnings."

They both laughed and the little man paid her the money. She rolled her eyes at Slocum, but he bent over, pulled her in close, and kissed her. She held her fingertips to her lips and her dark eyes opened wide. "This is going to be some evening," she whispered.

He adjusted his sombrero on his head. "What's next?"

"Food." She sounded taken aback. "I must go help them."

"No, Mama," her son said, coming up beside them. "I already took them the dishes of food you fixed. They can handle it. They saw you were busy with your guest."

In the late spears of sunshine coming over the mountain peaks above the village, she looked for celestial help, then quickly crossed herself.

"It'll be all right," Slocum assured her and moved her toward the open doors of the hall of the church across the square while her son ran ahead of them.

"You have made me forget my business here."

"I bet they make it fine. You needed some relaxation from all you do anyway."

"Oh, I don't work that hard. Except on special fiesta and church holidays. Where do you live, big man? I never saw you before in this country. You dress like a vaquero. You even walk like one. Why don't I know you?"

"I have never stopped long in this part of Sonora." He lowered his voice. "I'm looking for Valdez. The three fingers one."

Glancing down, he saw her shoulders shudder, then she looked up. "I know of him. I hate him too."

She led him through the food line, filling his tin plate so full, he wondered if he could eat half of what all she had piled on it. Then she pointed to a table for him to go sit at and said she would get them drinks.

Shaking his head in amusement at her motherliness, he obeyed her. One of the workers took his plate to find him a place to eat and about staggered under its weight as a joke, then set him up with his back to the wall. Another put a cloth napkin in his lap and warned him, "Do you know this woman who you carry around on your shoulders? She has a bad reputation—uh-oh, here she comes."

They all laughed at their joke.

Teresa put down the goblets. "All of you, leave this poor man alone. He needs his rest. He carried me all over the square."

"Oh." One of the older women put both of her hands on his shoulders and said, "This poor man's shoulders are so sore from carrying your fat body all over town that he may never walk again."

"Get out of here! All of you, so he will eat." She pushed and herded them away. "He is my guest."

One woman looked back. "For such a short woman, why do you need such a tall hombre?"

More laughter, but they were backing away from the spot where she put him, but not far enough away that the talking could not finish.

"Is none of your business. Now, go!"

"Oh, yes it is."

"Go."

When she rejoined him, he had to wipe the tears away, he'd laughed so hard watching her clear the space.

"Are you laughing at all my dumb friends?"

He shook his head, swung her around until she was standing beside him, and kissed her hard on the mouth. She turned away so her friends did not see her blink her eyes in reaction to his kiss.

Her arm around his neck, she whispered in his ear, "Hombre, you sure know how to—how do you say?—wake up my senses. Man, no one ever kissed me and curled my toes before."

"Good deal," he said, looking over the mountain of assorted cooked meats and things she'd selected for him to eat.

With her delicate fingers, she picked up a browned piece of meat and moved to put it in his mouth. "Here is something real good."

The mint flavor and rich meat taste caused his saliva glands to flood his mouth with moisture.

"That is mint and berry-flavored lamb."

"Best I've ever had. Can you tell me how to make that?"

"I can show you." This time she leaned in and kissed him on his still-greasy lips. With a cloth napkin, she cleaned his mouth of the shiny melted fat and then handed him the goblet. "Drink some wine. We make this here. I can see that we won't get much done tonight."

Amused, he shook his head at her words. "That would be a shame."

"I mean it." Then she got up, sat on the edge of the table beside his food, and began feeding him with her fingers.

One woman with a tray went by laughing. "Hombre, she is also a *bruja*. She will cast a spell on you."

"No, I won't." Teresa looked exasperated at her words.

He wrinkled his nose at her. "Go along, they are only having fun with you."

"I did not want anything to ruin our night together."

"I won't let anyone do that to you. I mean no one, but they are having fun with you."

Her dark brown eyes searched his own. "All right. No one will get my goat, huh?"

In a sweep, he hugged her. "Good idea."

The music played and they shuffled their feet in the dust, Slocum holding her tight to his waist until they stood as one. She must have decided that no one was paying them any attention and drew him back between the store and warehouse in the narrow space and then out the back way.

"I have a hammock where they won't ever find us. Is that all right?"

"You're the hostess. I will simply follow you."

Hugging his hip, she took him with her. "I wish I had known you ten years ago. When I was girl, not a widow."

"Nothing wrong with widows."

"Oh, to have had a great man like you take my virginity. That would have been a wonderful occasion."

"We can pretend it is your first night."

"Would you do that for me?"

"Damn right I will," he said and swept her up in his arms.

She began to cry. He stopped and under the stars looked at her wet face. "You all right?"

"I will try not to cry."

"You can cry afterward. Not now." He shook his head.

With a hard swallow, she nodded, looking up at him, and whispered, "Afterward—huh? Then I can cry?"

"Yes, I guess you can. Why then?" he asked, shifting her in his arms.

"'Cause then I will know my virginity is really gone forever." Under his arm, she waved for him to go to the right.

"You planned all day for this to happen to us tonight?" He could hardly believe she'd done all that on purpose.

"Is that bad?" she asked.

"Gads, no, girl. I'm excited as hell. How did you know I was coming?"

She wrinkled her nose at him. "I am a real *bruja*."

"Oh."

"Does it shock you that I am a witch?"

"No." He shook his head. She wasn't the first one he'd known who had those powers and she wouldn't be the last. Good witches fit in like good weather—wonderful. Bad ones were like stormy weather in Texas; they could be a killer tornado. Teresa was not an evil person. He trusted his personal insight when he was around supernatural people. She never gave him a moment of bad feelings, nor did he ever question her purposes toward him.

"Good, then my plans will work."

She led him down a narrow path into a dry wash, the shadowy light from the ceiling of stars overhead her only guide. At last they reached a hammock with a large mat on the ground, so they did not have to sit on the dirt to undress. Slocum recognized the back of her jacal—they were in Teresa's backyard. After he removed his gun belt, he rebuckled it and laid the harness on the ground. She stepped in close and began to unbutton his clothing.

With the kerchief from around his neck untied, his vest removed, and his shirt unbuttoned, her fingers ran familiarly through the fine hair on his chest. Then she pulled off his shirt. With his pants untied at the waist, she made him sit on his butt to remove his tall rawhide boots, then she pulled off his leather britches.

"Your outfit is new?" she asked and frowned in the night.

He nodded as she removed her blouse. She was taller than him when he dropped to his knees as she did a quick dance in a circle with her blouse high over her head.

Her pear-shaped breasts looked so inviting, shaking in his face, that he caught her and kissed them. Quickly she crushed his face to them.

"Wonderful, *mi amigo*."

"They taste like honey."

"You know that trick? Let some honey dry on your nipples, so when he tastes them, he thinks she secretes honey like milk for her child."

He laughed. He'd been tricked and treated to that sweetness before by that method, but it was a nice gesture for her to do it. He watched her wiggle out of the skirt and soon when she stood upright, he saw starlight dance on her flat stomach and her dark navel.

After he laid a kiss to her belly below her tits, she gathered his face up, bent over, and kissed him sweetly on the mouth. "Let's get in the hammock. A bed would have been better, but this was all I had to use."

"Those things get to be a problem."

"What is that?" she asked, climbing in the suspended bed.

"Those things we don't have and need."

She met him in the center and their mouths sought each other. Their lovemaking was much easier lying down than standing, and their rapid heartbeats and hard breathing soon had them struggling to get enough air.

Her small hand closed on his emerging erection and she quickly had a look-see down at its size and then shook her head. "Wow, you are powerfully big."

"We can go slow."

"Good," she said between erratic breathing.

His hands slipped over her body, testing, teasing, and playing with her like a boy with a new toy. The middle finger on his right hand slid through her coarse pubic hair, danced over her clit, and at last went inside her. Her juices were already flowing. She raised her butt up and spread her legs apart for his attention.

The word "paradise" kept filling his skull like a huge sign hand painted on the side of a rough board store. She pulled him over on top of her and he began his slow, easy exploration of her vagina with his throbbing hard-on.

From her contented face, her dark eyes shut underneath him, he could read the pleasure she was receiving from his efforts. Easy, easy—this was supposed to be her initial voyage into womanhood. He closed his eyes as she delivered herself to him.

Who cared about looking for Valdez? He'd found a real woman and was going to enjoy every moment of this breath-taking experience. His mouth flooded with his saliva, he swallowed hard past a knot and they went back to kissing. He was all the way inside her and the throbbing head of his dick rested against the end of the line.

Her short height made kissing her difficult but, as someone once told him, where there is will in fucking, there is a way to do it all. The notion amused him as he savored her lithe body and fiery energy—quite an eager *virginal* effort from her.

She opened her eyes, drew in a deep breath, and then closed them again, throwing her arms aside, as he really began to use her ass. The feeling that he had invaded someplace special filled his mind, and the fact that he intended to enjoy every inch of her sent him off to the stars. The real world faded to miles away.

There were lots of great women in his world to make love to, but this one was a fully wrapped package of blasting powder sticks with a sparkling, long-burning fuse. He didn't want their act to ever end, but on the other hand he longed for the great relief that blew out the end of his skin-tight erection and burned all the way up the tube.

The blast went off like an unexpected thunder boom from a quick-moving rain that slipped up on him unnoticed. She strained hard under him. The line of her jaw locked down tight, then she collapsed like a kite with no wind to hold it up.

Her hair was swept back from her face, and beads of shiny perspiration soon washed her cheeks as she shook her head in disbelief. "If every trip I had taken was that good, I'd be an addict to having you with me night and day."

He kissed her, moving down some in the hammock to be closer to her face. "And you are a widow woman living alone with your fine son in this small village. Why?"

"I guess I fear the unknown beyond this place. Here I am safe. There I would only be a *puta* living on the street with no place, no money, and sharing my body for two centavos with filthy drunks, no?"

"You paint such a bad picture. You are a real *bruja*. Use your powers—"

Gunshots out in the village square cut off his words. He bounded out of the hammock, grabbed his pants, and pulled them on in haste. Two more shots, and a woman screamed out there. He slung the holster over his shoulder and carried his six-gun in his fist.

"Oh, be careful. Don't let them kill you," she said, dressing as fast as he had.

Together they ran for the square. He could hear the frightened woman's shrill screams and children crying. At the edge of a building facing the square, he could see a man on a horse holding a kicking young girl over his lap, framed in the light of a Chinese lantern.

He aimed for the man's face, fired, and the bullet struck him in the nose. He went over backward off the horse. The girl fell with him but wasted no time scrambling to her bare feet and running for some sanctuary. Some older women caught her in their arms.

Two men wearing sombreros came out of the cantina, armed with pistols. "What is going on?" one shouted in Spanish.

Then, before anyone could answer, they swung their guns toward Slocum. He wasted no time and shot both of them. The pair crumpled to their knees after firing their pistols in the dirt.

"Where are the others?" he shouted in Spanish.

"By the store," a woman screeched and pointed that way. The warning cost her her own life. Someone gunned her down, but the killer caught the next hot lead fired from Slocum's gun muzzle. The shot caught the shooter and spun him around like top, and he teetered on his crossed boots before falling. A furious woman rushed out of the shadowy porch, swept up his gun, and shot him three times in the crotch at close range. His shrill voice cut the night. "No, no, someone stop her—"

But the hammer fell on a dud or an empty cylinder and she flung the weapon away. And went for him with a knife. "You won't rape anyone else's daughter. You *bastardo*—"

Other women physically pulled her back. Then three men on horseback tore through the crowd and Slocum was caught off guard, busy reloading. They went past him like screaming eagles, cross lashing their horses with long reins, and were gone into the night.

Teresa was busy checking on the victims. The shaken girl Slocum saved from the sure kidnapping was still trembling, and tears flooded her cheeks. Teresa hugged her to her chest and patted her back.

"She hurt?" Slocum asked, looking around.

"Only her pride. That was Valdez who rode out of here, right by you."

"I never got a good look at him. How many girls were raped?"

Teresa sadly shook her head. "We may never know. Some would only tell a priest what happened to them."

The padre was there, comforting and praying with several families in small groups.

A quiet man came and stood beside Slocum as he hugged Teresa. Aware of his presence, Slocum let go of her and spoke to him. "What can I do for you?"

"I came to shake your hand, *mi amigo*. My name is Diego. I have no money to pay you, but if I can ever help you, call on me."

"Gracias." Slocum felt comforted by the sincere person. Others soon came forth to line up, the women to kiss him on the cheek, the men to shake his hand.

"They are giving you the key to their city," Teresa said in a soft voice.

"What will it open?" he asked her aside.

"Oh, my jacal, I guess."

"Good enough."

She nodded toward the cantina. "The men want to buy you a beer over at the cantina."

"That would be nice."

She shoved her flat hand against his muscle-corded belly and shook her head at him. "I will be in my hammock when you can get away from them."

"Keep your fire hot. I won't stay long, darling."

She blushed and pushed him to go across the square. "Make sure it is my bed that you find later."

He nodded that he heard her request and strode off to the saloon, stopping several times to hear some words of gratitude from the villagers. Inside the saloon, a shout went up when he appeared. They all smiled, and more men moved in to get a chance to shake his hand. Someone brought him a beer. He thanked them and told them he was only there to help them run off the bad ones.

After a short while of listening to their problems with the wild bunch, he agreed they needed more protection and thanked them for the beer. Out under the stars, he crossed the square and reached the small, dark street that led behind the storefronts.

"Señor?" a woman's voice called to him.

"Si?"

"Why do you bed that *bruja*? There are several nice women who would welcome you to their bed."

He tipped his hat. *"Gracias*, but do not worry about me."

"I will worry about your sanity too, señor. I will burn candles to save your life. You are in deep trouble going to her."

He went on, not seeing Teresa's accuser. She was mumbling Hail Marys for him and he smiled to himself as he went on. At Teresa's place, he stopped in the shadows and waited in case he was being followed. No one came.

In the backyard by the hammock, he began to undress. She awoke and stretched her arms. "You did not stay long?"

"I was anxious to get back to you."

She sat up and fluffed her hair. "Mmm, that sounds good."

Undressed, he eased himself onto the swinging bed. In seconds, her warm skin and tempting body were against his wind-chilled form. Under the thick, woven, cotton blanket they snuggled, and the temperature began to rise between the two of them.

His quickly rising erection slipped into the entry of her vagina as she kissed him wildly. A quick notion pricked him: *Why did they think she was a witch?*

17

The next morning, he awoke to a fighting cock's bragging that the sun was coming up. Careful not to dump a sleeping Teresa out on the ground, he eased out of the hammock. He needed to get on with his search for Valdez. Dressed, he studied the scratching game birds taking apart the horse turds, looking for undigested grain in them. The lead male was crowing, then scratching and searching among his brown-colored females for something edible. Tough animals to even survive in such a harsh land. Common breeds of birds would have died by this time.

Teresa tackled his waist, then raised her face and tossed her hair back for him to kiss her. "What will we do today?"

"I must go look for Valdez."

"Will you come back to me?"

"If I can. There is another of these outlaws who is hiding behind Old Man Clanton's skirts who needs to be taken care of as well as Valdez."

"I will look for you to ride back. Come with me. We will have some breakfast and coffee before you leave. Mia is cooking in the square."

"I'll saddle my horse and join you there."

"No, Ronaldo can saddle him. I want you with me—to show

off. Wait here one minute. I will go get my son to saddle that fine horse."

Maybe he would have time to quiz her about her powers? Soon she returned and snuggled close to his waist.

"Ronaldo will have your horse ready when we are through with breakfast." So she guided him to the square, where the woman Mia cooked food and fresh tortillas.

Teresa ordered their food and then poured two tin cups of coffee for them.

Slocum gave her the money to pay the woman for their food. Teresa frowned at the coins he gave her. "Too much, hombre."

"No, she can use it."

With an "oh well" shrug, she went over to hand Mia the money. Mia dumped the coins in between her cleavage and turned to grin at him. "*Gracias*, señor."

An hour later, he kissed Teresa good-bye and left the village. Several residents told him how to find Valdez, but they all told him to watch out, that he and his compadres were mean, tough men with no hearts for anyone. Slocum rode southwest into an unfamiliar desert country that he felt was as tough as the outlaw residents.

The tall cactus was more like tall tubes than the Arizona saguaros with their balanced arms. Great beds of pad cactus caused him to detour as he followed the game trails rather than a road the outlaws might use. He wanted to simply scout around the region and learn all he could about the man he sought.

Midday, he found a windmill, a tank, and a squaw shade with some brush corrals. A short, pregnant young woman came out carrying a baby and asked what he was looking for.

"A drink for my horse and myself."

"The water is there. You are far from the roads, señor. Who do you look for?"

"Maybe I wish to be away from the roads." He dropped from the saddle, removed his hat, and wiped the perspiration on his sleeve.

"When did you eat last?" she asked with concern written on her face.

"This morning."

"When you get through with the water, come to my shade. I can fix you some food." She waited for his reply.

"Thank you. I can pay you."

She paused, hoisted the baby up. "If you can, that is fine."

He watered the horse and drank from the pipe. The water had a salty flavor. Then he tread the soft, sandy ground under his boots on his way to hitch his horse on the smooth, worn wooden rack. His hat off, he ducked to go under the edge of a palm frond roof and straightened once he was in her house.

She rose up and smiled at him, filling a plate with some long-cooked brown beans. She put two folded tortillas on top of them and then told him to sit on a blanket. With the plate put in his hands, she gathered her skirt to sit down close beside him.

"Do you have a woman somewhere?" she asked.

He thanked her for the meal and said, "No wife."

"You are not a Mexican, yet you still dress like one."

He glanced up and smiled at her. "Maybe I'm a ghost?"

"No." She shook her head, amused at his words. "You are too much a real hombre to be a ghost. They are like smoke. You are too *grande* to be one of them." She laughed at his answer.

"Maybe I am the spirit Kokopelli that the Indians speak of?"

"You may be him all right." She giggled. "But you are a big one if you are him. What is your name?"

"Slocum. What is yours?"

"Lucia. Slow-cum?" She drew his name out. "Does it mean anything?"

"Does Lucia mean anything?" He used a piece of a tortilla to dip out his beans. They tasted better than he'd expected.

"It means I get lonely out here." She dropped her gaze to her belly, which showed her condition.

"Where is the baby's father?"

"He needed money and went to Arizona to find some work."

"You have no one to help you here?"

She squinted her eyes, looking away, and shook her head. "He promised to be back before I go into labor."

"Is there no one close by to help you?"

She wrinkled her nose. "I will be fine. I guess I am—how do you say?—lonely."

"It gets where it's good to talk to someone after a while, doesn't it?" He nodded, emphasizing his words. Company was a rewarding thing after being alone for an extended while.

"I figured you'd know what bothers me the most."

"Not having someone to hold you?" he asked.

"Ah, *sí*." She scooted a little closer to him on the blanket.

"I am looking for a man called Valdez who rides in this country."

"I don't know him. Is he a good man?"

"No."

"Why do you want him then?"

"He raped a young woman in the mountains. He's a cruel man."

She put both her hands on his shoulder and pushed down some on him. "Am I too ugly to—"

"To make love to? No."

"Good, then I will undress for you, if you will not make fun of me."

"I would never do that to you." He twisted to watch her stand up and untie the strings on her skirt waist. She shed the bottom of her clothing and exposed light brown legs and her small butt. Then she shed the blouse over her head. Her small, full breasts were capped by brown nipples and appeared to be full of milk for the little one asleep in the crib.

Finished with undressing, she pulled on his arm to get him to get up and go with her. He followed her to where she must have slept on a pallet. With trembling hands, she tried to undo his gun belt. He moved to assist her when the heavy holster was at last in her hands.

They both stopped when they heard the sounds: Horses were coming. She swept up her clothing and hastily began to dress. "Who is it?"

His gun belt around his waist again, he shook his head, adjusting it. "I'll go see."

He rushed out and saw three riders coming through the desert brush. He holstered his Colt, jerked the rifle out of its scabbard, and headed for some higher ground. He ran straight through some low cactus pads, the plants penetrating his right foot through his boots, but he saw the puffs of the men's pistol shots. Valdez must have found him, intent on revenge for the shootings last night. He shouldered the rifle, took aim, and shot the rider on the right off his horse. He smoothly reloaded the rifle with the lever action and swung the sight to the left. Then, with deliberate aim, he slammed a bullet in the second rider's horse in the center, and the horse went down, its rider tumbling out of the saddle. The target proved hard to catch, which was why he chose the animal. The rider disappeared into a dry wash and out of sight.

No telling how badly the one thrown off the horse was hurt, but he'd scrambled after his buddy into the wash. The cactus spines in Slocum's right boot hurt as he headed back to his horse for more bullets. The limp slowed him down.

"Who is it?" Lucia asked, huddling with the baby in her arms.

"I think it is Valdez. I got one of them." He put the pistol bullets from his saddlebags in his pants pockets, reloaded the rifle, and looked around for any sight of them. "You need to get behind a wall."

"There are some old ruins over there." She pointed to them.

"Go to them. Take some water and something to shade you and the baby."

She nodded and went back under the palm roof. He considered using the horse to go find them, but decided against it—he couldn't afford for them to shoot his horse out from under him as he'd done to one of them. With the foot hurting him more, he hobbled to the west of the squaw shade to try to find the location of the two outlaws still alive.

Two shots came at him from the chaparral. He saw the puffs of gun smoke, but he never saw the shooters, and the gray clouds soon drifted from the source on the hot wind. They were too far away for pistols to be effective. Then he saw them riding double, trying to get away. There was only time for one shot; aiming his rifle, he took the horse out. The bay went down, spilling both riders, but Slocum knew they were too far away for him to catch. They could reach cover before he could close in on them.

The pain in his foot forced him to turn back. The woman and baby needed to be guarded. He limped back to the squaw shade and she waved for him to join her in the ruins.

"You get them?" she asked when he got to her.

"Not all of them, just one. Two more got away."

"Too hot down there." She handed him a goatskin water bag.

He nodded to her in gratitude. He removed the cork and took a drink. It was wet; that was the best he could say about the contents. Nothing to cool his mouth, but simply wet it.

"They still out there?" she asked.

"Yes. I shot their horses."

"Then they will come when it is dark to try to get yours."

"If they're still alive."

"Don't you feel that cactus in your boot?" She frowned at him over her discovery.

"It hurts, but I haven't had any time to deal with it."

"I will need to find some sticks to get it off. You sit down."

"Yes, ma'am." He dropped his butt to the blanket rug, set the rifle down beside him, and waited for her to select some sticks from her cooking fuel and return.

On her knees before him, she used the sticks to squeeze the ball of needles and ripped the thing away. He flinched at the pain, but she ignored him and took the ball to her ashes to burn it. Then she hurried back and carefully pulled his boot off. That hurt too.

She began to pull the obvious spines out of the leather. Each one had a tiny barb on the end, so they didn't come out easily. After that she felt inside and removed some more sticking in the sole.

"Take off your sock," she said, looking at him in concern, and waited for him to ease away the sticker-filled stocking. When it was off, she worked on getting the spines out of his sore foot. He winced every time she removed one, and also as she tried to clean the sock of them. There must be a million in the sock, he decided. She was working on the others in his tender bare foot. Sweat ran out from under his hatband, and he wiped it off on his sleeve.

"This is damn tough work," he mumbled.

With a toss of her hair, she shook her head. "They can poison you. I am getting all of them that I can. Some we will break off, and when they fester, we can use a needle on them."

"Oh, good," he said, imagining that. More sharp pain. "I need to look around. Those men may be sneaking up on us." She agreed. He picked up his rifle and went to the edge of the ruins on one bare foot.

He had to get down on his knees to see out around the edge, and he looked all around, watching for any sign—nothing. His bare foot felt numb. Getting up and down and going over the rough ground was a pain-filled torture.

She guided him back, then made him lie down. "When will they try for us?"

"Sundown, and they'll come from the west."

"Why from the west?"

"So the sun will be in our eyes."

"*Sí.*" She made a concerned face at him, then the baby cried and she scrambled to go see about him.

He worked on his foot some more. The spines scratched his fingertips as he tried to pull them out. For the rest, he'd have to wait until they festered like she said. His boot without the sock might be better, since the material of the sock was embedded with them. He used his hand to search inside the boot. He found more spines, and with her small fingers, she extracted them.

She fed him some beans and the baby some mashed ones. The boot back on his foot felt funny without a sock, but he gritted his teeth against the pain of what felt like a thousand spines still in his skin down there. He scouted around, watered his horse, unsaddled him, and put him in a corral. There was the bait—the good horse.

With no idea how hurt those two were from getting unseated from their horses, he knew good and well they weren't going to leave on foot when he had a horse. He felt they were watching him from some secure place. Good. He'd meet them head-on.

The day took forever to fall off somewhere into the distant Gulf of California. Watching the bleeding western sky, he lay on his belly with his rifle in his hand. The squaw shade was on a high point, and anyone approaching it had no cover for three hundred feet. That made it more defensible.

Lucia came over and lay down beside him on her side. The baby was asleep. "Any sign of them?"

He shook his head.

She fingered something like a small leather string and did not look at him. "I know you have been busy with those two bastards. You have not forgotten about me?"

"No, but we better hold off on that until I settle with them."

"Oh, I understand. I didn't want you to leave until—well, you know."

"You have been lonely, haven't you?"

Tears ran down her face in the last of twilight. "You don't know how good it felt to have someone to talk to."

He nodded, his attention centered on the darkening country outside the shade. Then he listened hard and put his finger on her mouth. He'd heard a noise—the sound of something under someone's foot snapping.

"They are coming," she whispered and sucked in her breath.

"Real easy," he said in her ear and kissed her on the cheek. She quickly clutched his head and kissed him hard.

His hand tightened on the pistol grip. He heard the sound of more soles scraping, and the brittle grass complained. His heart pounded hard beneath his throat.

18

Time for him to move away from Lucia. He rose and waved for her to stay. In the dim light, he saw her cross herself. They were coming across the open ground. One of them was dragging his leg; obviously he had been injured. The other person, not looking too steady, held a rifle.

"Halt," Slocum ordered.

The rifle bearer shot from the hip and the .45 in Slocum's hand exploded. His target screamed. Slocum drew a bead on the other silhouette and shot at him. The orange flash of that man's pistol went off into the dirt. Slocum shot him again.

"Did you get them?" Lucia whispered as the baby began to cry.

"I'm not certain. You and the baby stay here until I know for sure."

She agreed, quietly comforting the child in her arms.

His injured foot hurt to walk on. He stood outside the shade in the twilight and reloaded his handgun. With that task complete and the pistol cocked, he started for the two downed outlaws. When he drew closer, he heard the rifleman complaining in Spanish.

He crossed the ground quickly and kicked the rifle away with his sore foot, pointing his six-gun at the man. "You Valdez?"

"Who are you, hombre?"

"My name is Slocum. I'm the man who shot you. I've been gunning for you for what you did to a young woman named Nana in the mountains."

"I never did anything to any woman."

Slocum reached down and grabbed his wrist. Then he jerked the three-fingered claw up in the air to see the outline. "Yes. You are one of the bastards who raped her."

"I'm bleeding to death. Do something for me."

"If you were drowning in a well, I wouldn't do anything but piss on you."

"You are not human," Valdez complained.

"Yeah, I am. Outlaws like you never earned one tear from me."

"I hope you burn in hell."

"You will first." Slocum found the other one on the ground, breathing his last. Satisfied, he gathered their weapons and took them back to the shade. He had no problem turning his back and leaving the two men to die. Valdez would soon expire, and his compadre would slip away even sooner.

"Are they dead?" she whispered.

"They will be soon."

He could see in the little light left that she was holding herself tightly. He hugged her to him. "The baby is all right?"

"He is fine. The shots upset him, but he is asleep now."

"This is about over."

She stood on her toes and kissed him hard on the mouth. He nodded, squeezing her warmly, then went back to check on the two dying men. Valdez's compadre had no pulse, and neither did Valdez. He closed the outlaw's blue eyes and stood up to look at the array of stars overhead.

One more rapist to find—Gorman. That might require more strength than he had; if that rapist stayed inside Old Man Clanton's fortress, Slocum might not be able to get to him. If Gorman ever left the fortified ranch, he'd sure enough run him down. But he had better things to do right now than to worry about that worthless scum.

He ducked at the roof edge and came under the shade, and once well inside he straightened.

She hissed at him.

"Coming. They're no problem to anyone anymore."

She raised the light blanket for him to join her in the shadowy light. He pulled off his boots—the right one carefully—and quickly shed his clothing. The gun holster was rebuckled and set beside where he knelt to join her on the pallet.

Under the light covers, she pressed her ripe body and belly against him and her hot mouth sought his. She was so hungry for his affection, he hoped that she did not bust her heart in her anxious search for some escape from her loneliness. Her hand soon clutched his half erection, moved him on top of her, and started it inside her vagina. In seconds, he pumped his hard-on upward into her tunnel. They were coupled and the rise in her belly was easily surmountable. Both were pounding away in matched efforts with no sense of time or place in their wild abandon.

Their hard breathing sounded like wind-broke horses gasping for air. Time and again their hungry mouths fed on each other. Then they sped up, hunching each other until at last, deep in his sac, lightning struck his balls and a volcano shot off into her depths. Depleted, they both collapsed, with him being careful not to crush her.

"Oh." She huffed. "Oh, how wonderful you are. I never felt like this before."

"Maybe you weren't so lonely back then. But I have never felt so excited in my life. Some man needs you." Her small breasts rose and fell between them; she was still short of breath. They lay on their sides and recovered. Her hands could not resist jacking him off.

They kissed and honey seeped from her mouth into his. They slept some, then woke up and had more involvement again. The third time they awoke, his balls screamed for relief, and he hugged her to his chest until his erection grew and she put him in from the backside.

The baby woke them at dawn. She quickly half dressed and

soon had her son in her arms. A rose light of dawn crept over the distant sawtooth mountains. After she fed her child and set him in his cradle, she made Slocum some breakfast of fresh tortillas and coffee.

He finished the meal and looked up at her. "I'm going to bury those outlaws in a dry wash today."

"Then you will leave me?"

"I will stay another night—give my foot a chance to heal up some more. Then I must go."

"I savvy, but I will cry when you go away." She pulled his face down to kiss him and put his hand on her exposed breast. He eased it over the tight form. He really felt sorry for her, but he could not take her with him, nor could he stay. But he would send a couple of pack mule loads of supplies back for her.

His morning was spent saddling his horse and dragging the corpses by their feet with a rope tied on the saddle horn to a place where he could collapse a dry wash wall to cover them. Then he used a short-handled shovel to dig out the wall and let it fall in on the still bodies. He limped through it all on his still-sore right foot.

When he finished, he bathed and washed his clothing in a rock-mortar stock tank. Lucia came to talk to him while his clothing dried. She slipped into his arms and smiled confidently up at him. "I have you captured."

"For now, girl, you have me."

"You must be tired. After all that work, take a siesta. I will bring your clothing when they are dry."

He agreed, kissed her, and went to lie down for a nap. A pounding headache racked his brain when she woke him. One look and she told him to sit there.

"Do you have a headache?" she asked, peering into his eyes.

He held his head and agreed, not certain about the cause. The hammerlike thumps made him wonder what was wrong inside his skull.

"I can make you some willow bark tea and stop it. Can you hold the baby? He is crying," she said and went to get him.

Slocum took the small fellow in his arms to hold and talk to him. He soon settled down, and she busied herself making the tea with boiling water. In a few minutes, she took back her son and left him holding a large tin cup of the brew.

The boy, who she called José, stopped his snuffling once she changed his diaper.

With the cup in his hand, Slocum blew on the brew so it did not scald his tongue. He was anxious to get the medicine into his system to stop the pounding in his head, not to mention the throbbing in his foot.

"What should we do with their guns and their saddles?" she asked.

"You may sell them or your man can sell them. They will bring some money."

She nodded that she understood. "Did they have any money?"

"Not much. I only found a few dollars on them." He dug out the handful he had collected and tried to give it to her.

"No, you will need it to find that other *bastardo*." But his insistence prevailed and she took it.

A while after he drank the tea, his headache began to recede, and his aching foot felt a little better too. Lucia decided it was time to dig out the rest of the cactus spines still in his foot, which were red and starting to fester. She got out her sewing needle and carefully worked the leftover spines out of his foot, though each one made him wince in pain. Finally, she was done, and she washed his foot, then sent him to lie down on the pallet.

When the sun set, they made love twice and finally went to sleep with her naked body clinging to his under the blanket that kept them warm in the cool night. Slocum dreaded the ride back and leaving her openness and the generous gift of her young body. Even pregnant she was a love child with tender, sweet ways not many women ever shared with a man. Like they were afraid to expose themselves and then be hurt.

He rode off the next morning, heading north and feeling sad to have to part from Lucia. He stopped in St. Thomas, arranged to send supplies to Lucia, and spent the night with Teresa. She left him little opportunity to sleep, trying hard to prove to him that she was the best woman for him in all of Mexico and that he should stay there with her. But he left the village and her asleep to wander north the next day until midafternoon, when he found some cottonwood shade to sleep in for a few hours. He woke in the night, gnawed on some hard beef jerky, and rode on north under the stars in a groggy state. Late the next day he reached the Peralta Springs Ranch, where he planned to cross the border.

The good food there revived him some and he went to bed early, realizing the handsome older woman Carmellia would probably join him in the night. He was not disappointed, for she came to his hammock after midnight.

He was awake as she hurried to undress beside his swing. She whispered, "Oh, I wondered for how long you would be gone."

Then she slipped into his arms like she belonged there. Her fine, pear-shaped breasts rested on his chest when she reached under and inserted him in her vagina. His erection was stiff enough by then to stay inside of her, and she squirmed on top of him. Then she bent over and kissed him hard. "Oh, you are ready so quick. What a pleasure you are to me."

She hunched at his growing sword and let out small sighs of pleasure. "Oh, how I have dreamed you would come back to visit me."

In dreamland with her riding his shaft, he kneaded her breasts and she closed her eyes in the starlight at the pleasure she enjoyed from being in his arms. Then they changed positions and he climbed on top of her, poking his way to heaven atop her flat belly and savoring every moment of his capture. Their pelvic bones smashed their pubic hair in a gritty grinding as he sought her depths. On and on they went until at last he felt on the brink and he signaled to her he was about to close on this session. She wrapped her legs around him and strained, then they both came—hard—and fell out into a world of faint, free-falling through space.

Excited at her successful ending, she smothered him with kisses and slipped off the hammock. "I must go now, big hombre."

In minutes, she was dressed, the shawl covering her head. He studied the silhouette of her figure standing over him against the starry sky before she kissed him again, and he nodded in approval. "God bless you."

Then she left, silent as the night wind that swept across his face. Whew. She was some woman and he was the fortunate receiver of her love. Damn, he knew some neat women in his world. He wondered if the man he had hired had delivered Lucia her supplies. Now maybe she and the baby had better nutrition than simply beans all the time.

He slept some more before the ranch came alive in the pre-dawn. Where in the hell would he find Gorman? A question he'd asked himself a hundred times since he started out of Sonora for the Arizona Territory. Still a half-day's ride out of Tombstone, he saddled his horse. Several vaqueros spoke about the handsome gelding.

"Ah," he agreed. "He not only looks good, but he's as tough as that old Roman-nosed goose I rode over here a few weeks ago."

The men laughed with lots of "*Si*'s." They were a tough lot. Desert vaqueros were a brand all their own; they were always floured in dust and ready for fun. They could rope better than most any ranch hands in the West. And they used riatas, the braided strands cut full-length from a raw steer hide and lubricated with sheep fat. They dally roped because they needed to let the rope slip on the saddle horn when roping big stock and avoid the full weight slamming to the end. He loved to simply watch them catch hind hooves at roundup.

He also liked that they accepted him as one of them. The feeling of belonging there was good. To be in a fraternity with such tough men was an honor few gringos could brag about.

After breakfast, he rode on to Carla Hunton's cat house in Tombstone, where he planned to headquarter and from there look for Gorman. Hopefully he wasn't at Old Man Clanton's ranch, but Slocum needed to find out either way. Someone in the city knew the outlaw's whereabouts and he wanted the address and to get this business over and be gone.

There was always the fear that someone would get drunk somewhere and be asked, "Where's this Slocum at?" and that someone would spill the beans to the bounty hunter asking. "I seed him last week in Tombstone." That would be all it took, and some kid looking for a name for himself or some gritty old reward finder would ride over and jump him. Old or young, they all wanted the price on his head and the fame for whatever two cents that was worth.

Slocum dismounted at the livery and boarded his horse. Then he walked the four blocks across town to Carla's place, packing his saddlebags and rifle. When he slugged up the six stairs to the porch, the front door popped open, and one of the girls in a white shift held her finger to her lips for him to be quiet. He removed the big sombrero and tiptoed inside the doorway. Out of the hot sun, he set his bags and rifle down, then gave her the hat and removed his spurs, leaning against the jamb. He'd already removed his chaps and left them at the livery on his saddle. She took his spurs, returned his hat, and led him to the stairs.

"Oh, Carla. Oh, Carla."

"What's wrong with you girls now—" Her eyes bugged out and, grasping the rail on the second floor, she looked shocked to see him standing there with his big hat in hand. "Slo—cum! You—you're back so soon." Then she sped down the stairs with her arms out for him, gushing with excitement.

They met about halfway and he swept her up in his arms. The girls applauded and she waved them away before she kissed him.

"How long have you been here?" she asked, breaking away from his mouth.

"Long enough to board my horse and walk over here." He looked back down to see about his things and set her down.

"They can store them. Come with me."

With her dragging him inside her bedroom, he noted the afternoon wind had the filmy curtains waving behind the open windows. The wind felt fresh as she turned her back for him to undo the buttons on the back of her dress—small buttons that were in a line and not easy to undo. But he wanted her out of the dress and she wanted out maybe worse than he did.

"I should have taken a bath before I came here," he said, slipping his hands in under the dress material and cupping both of her breasts. "I probably smell like a horse."

"I couldn't care less. I've been thinking about you all week long." Then he let go and she turned to face him. The dress spilled to her waist, exposing her exquisite, pear-shaped breasts. Like a hungry lioness, she hugged him tight, and her tongue sought his tonsils. They finally moved apart and she stepped out of the gown. It was a magnificent departure only a real professional woman could attain. Anyone else would have stumbled around to get free of her slips, but not Carla. Her moves not only attracted him, but the slender turn of her hips and legs made his heart trip a beat under his rib cage. She was a goddess of something.

Sheets thrown aside on the mattress, she eased herself toward the head of the bed. Then in place, she raised her parted knees with her arms held out for him get between them and on top of her natural saddle. Her hand slipped the head of his rising sword in through the lips of her vagina, and she raised her butt in anticipation of her probe coming through her ring of fire. Connection complete, he started the steam-engine piston drive that quickly heightened her breathing. Flying like soaring eagles, they rode the updrafts to new heights and then swooped down to where the splash of the rapids dampened their feathers. The two quickly dried in their own world of seeking success until his efforts culminated in a great explosion inside her. They fell into a pile like discarded beer bottles behind a saloon.

"Oh my God," she cried out, closing her blue eyes and straining at the hands on her hips. "It was worth waiting for—you devil you. What now?"

He shook his head. "I have no idea. A meal in bed? A bath? A siesta? More of the same?"

They had to twist and squirm around to get together to kiss again. "A siesta first?" he asked.

"Ah, *sí*," she said and snuggled against him. "When must you leave?"

"Two or three days. I need to find him—this Gorman guy."

"What if I hire two good detectives and they can find him while you rest with me?"

"I need to find him. I don't want him to run away. I'll find him and you won't hardly miss me."

She looked at the ceiling for some help, then smiled and shook her head. "It is your business. I just want to keep you."

He lightly tousled her hair and she closed her eyes in their bed of flesh. They kissed like starving lovers and drew together for more.

Later, after a hot bath, he shaved while she saw about her business downstairs, returning still amazingly fresh-looking. A take-charge woman who could silence a fight between her employees, handle a tough, out-of-hand customer, and keep the peace in the place just by pointing her finger like a sword. The situation amused him: a refined lady as well as one who made love without any social restraints.

They ate supper in her apartment. There was sliced beef roast, mashed potatoes, fresh green beans, some hot French bread, a dry wine, and a cinnamon-flavored apple pie. Slocum was in a clean suit of clothing; he left his Mexican clothes to be cleaned by her domestic help and ready for him to change into again when he had to. His cowboy gear was hanging up in Carla's closet.

He slipped out after dark and made a tour of the town. Hamby Cox was closing his café and looked up with a frown until he discovered the man was Slocum. Cox invited him inside and closed the front door, pulling the curtains to secure some privacy for them.

When they were both seated on stools at the counter, Cox began with, "Gorman was seen in Charleston this week. He may think you're dead."

"Good, so long as he keeps on thinking that. Valdez is where he belongs: in hell. No one else will find out about it, but we know he is not here on the earth any longer."

"Ike has made some boasts that he had you killed."

"Whiskey talk. He may be shocked at my reappearance."

Hamby laughed. "You knew they found the buckboard remains and the guards' bodies. I guess you did that before you went back south of the border."

Slocum agreed. "So, we don't know if Gorman is still in Charleston, down in Mexico at his own place, or sticking close to the Old Man's place?"

"I also heard he was in on a big stage robbery down in Sonora. Hard to miss a short, fat white guy with a scar over his right eye."

"Yes and that's good."

"What will you do next?" Hamby asked, drumming his fingernails on the counter. "And what can I do?"

"Help me find him."

"I'll try my damnedest."

They shook hands and Hamby let him out the back door to blend back into the night crowd of miners, cowboys, ranch hands, gamblers, and con men. Slocum found Virgil Earp, the only one of the Earps that Slocum had any truck with, and they spoke softly in a back booth of the Oriental Saloon.

"I haven't seen Gorman in weeks. I guess you sent him into hiding." A mild smile on Earp's straight lips and a momentary luster in his eyes expressed the stone-faced marshal's pleasure at any discomfort for a member of the Clanton gang.

"I guess you know I want him for his wanton rape of a young woman in Mexico."

Earp nodded and folded his hands on the table, then undid them when he spoke. "There is a lot more clearing out of the deadwood needed around here. Felons running around scot-free. I can't tell you a thing you probably don't know already. But if I hear anything, I'll find you."

Slocum thanked him. They shook hands and parted. Slocum checked a few more saloons, but there was no sign or word of Gorman in any of them. From a vantage point, he looked over the drunk Cowboys staying overnight at the O.K. Corral. They were too drunk, and besides puking, they made little sense to him. He went back to Carla's open arms.

"Did you learn anything tonight?" she asked as they undressed in the dimly lit bedroom.

"No. Nothing worth spending four hours away from you for. So I'd just as soon make up for lost time."

Naked as Eve, she slipped into his arms and sighed. "That sounds wonderful."

19

In the middle of the night, someone knocked on Carla's door and woke them. She told him to stay, got out of bed, and put on her bathrobe to answer the knock. "Probably for me."

Still half asleep, he lay back down to await her word. She closed the door and turned to him. He sat up fast at her words. "Cleo says a man downstairs needs to talk to you about Gorman."

Getting up, he started to put his legs into his pants. "Did he give her his name?"

"She said no."

"I'll find it out," he said to dismiss their concerns.

"It could be a trap," Carla said.

He finished dressing and strapped on his six-gun. He kissed her and swept up his hat. "I'll be back whenever."

"Oh, you be very careful."

From the second floor, he looked down at the stranger standing in the living room. His brown hat was unfamiliar from the crown view. Something was wrong. This was no ordinary person standing in Carla's parlor. He was halfway down the flight when the man spun around and his hand went for his gun.

Slocum drew and fired first, and the man was struck in the chest. The percussion of the two pistols going off blew out the lamps, and boiling gun smoke filled the room. The assassin's bullet went into the hardwood floor. A black domestic ran in and, with a pail of water, slushed out any fire the shot might have caused. Coughing hard, she ran back into the kitchen. Slocum was already out the front door, and, seeing a fleeing rider racing off into the night, he decided to hold his shot at him.

"Was there another?" Carla asked from the porch. "Who was he?"

"One holding the horses. Both were damn dumb fools."

"You didn't know them?"

"Not the one I shot. I couldn't see who the other was." He felt burnt to a crisp by their intrusion. Whoever sent the man to kill him needed to be killed himself.

"Cleo has gone for the law."

"Good. None of us will get much sleep tonight," he said, holstering his Colt and climbing the stairs.

The girls were all talking at once in the parlor. Someone had put a rag rug over the dead gunman's body and removed his spurs so they did not scar the hardwood floor. The dust-free band where the spur straps once shielded the leather of the boots was obvious. Who was he? Someone would know him. What next?

Pretty damn bold to come right into Carla's house and ask for him. No telling what that man had been thinking. Slocum would probably never know who'd hired him. Might have had to get fortified on whiskey. No telling—Marshal White and Virgil Earp came scrambling up the porch steps.

A portly man, White knelt down in the parlor and lifted the rug. "You know him, Virgil?"

The taller man glanced over at the corpse and shook his head. "Never seen him before. He call you out, Slocum?"

"He told the night girl, Cleo, he had a message for me. I was asleep. He was pacing the floor when I came down the stairs and I wondered who was under that hat. Got halfway down and he drew his gun. I figured he wasn't here to cut fish bait unless it was me."

White's mouth made a sardonic move to one side. He shook

his head when Doc Myers came in, bag and all. "You're too late. He's dead."

"Hell, White, I could have slept."

"Doc, we'll need a report for a coroner's jury." White took his hat off when Carla brought them all cups of steaming coffee from the kitchen. White and Earp thanked her.

Slocum and Carla didn't get back to their bed until a rosy pink had dawn climbed up over the Chiricahuas. John Doe was on a slab at Gleason's Funeral Home. Both lawmen had returned to their office and jail.

Slocum yawned, undressed, fell back on the sheet, and tried to sleep some as the town woke up.

When he awoke midmorning, he learned that they had found out the dead man's name was Rod Pearson, formerly of Texas. Carla sat on the edge of the bed and rubbed Slocum's bare back with both hands.

"Who hired him?" she asked, leaning in hard on his back.

"He was a new Cowboy, I reckon. Damn, that feels so good, you could do it for another couple of hours."

"You want some food?"

"I guess I could use some."

"I'll go pull a cord and they'll fix you something. I think they're spoiling you anyway."

"I need to be spoiled."

She laughed and kissed the side of his face. "All you need is me under you and you'd be set."

He pushed up on his arms to sit upright. "Maybe. We'll have to try that later."

"You better, after the mess we had to clean up downstairs."

"You could've awakened me. I'd have helped you."

She chuckled and hugged him. "By the time we got started doing that, you were already sawing a log."

Damn, he had slept hard. "I better get dressed. Anything else happening today?"

She shook her head. "Just another day at the store."

Damn shame, but he knew the gunman from the night before came from Clanton, even as an unknown. Slocum had been lucky; that bastard could have put him down right there. Hell, there wasn't a safe place in the world anymore for him to hide. How did they know about his arrangement with Carla? Spied on him was the answer. *Well, Old Man Clanton, your days may be numbered too.* But that horse-stealing Ike was the next one needing his ears notched like a hog. Maybe he'd find him in Charleston.

20

In the late afternoon he rode south to Charleston, where they crushed the silver ore from the mines. Ike sometimes hung around there in a Mexican bar. Slocum planned to pin the sumbitch's ears back permanently for the attempt to kill him if he found him.

Slocum stopped first at the Los Olivos Cantina. He hitched his horse in the shade of some cottonwoods on the bank of the San Pedro River. He took off his hat, wiped his gritty forehead on his sleeve, and replaced the Stetson. Then he went inside the cantina to see what he could find out.

"Ah, señor." A familiar Hispanic man sitting at a table and wearing a big sombrero rose and waved him over.

"So you killed another one of them *bastardos* last night at Carla's house. You must have a lot of enemies." Henry Castro said, rising to his feet and shaking Slocum's hand. Castro ran cattle on both sides of the border and tangled often with the Clantons, who conveniently gathered a few head of Castro's cattle every time they took a herd across his land to the army or the Indian Agencies. That occurred several times a year.

"Have a seat, my compadre, and tell me about this assassin." He reached over and turned out a wooden chair for Slocum to use.

Slocum looked around the dimly lit cantina, then sat, satis-fied no one in the place looked threatening. He took the chair that put his back to the wall.

"How have you been, Henry?"

"Except for them Cowboys stealing my cattle, I'm fine. Who was this shooter I heard about?"

"Some Texan named Pearson. Five foot six, and he looked like a mad bulldog when he finally faced me, ready to draw. I never saw him before, and his partner outside Carla's place rode off hard into the night. No one saw his face."

"I wondered if you knew him. They tell me that worthless Valdez is dead."

"If he owes you money, write him off."

Castro laughed and sat back to appraise him. "I bet the old man sent him, huh?"

Slocum shook his head. "That was not a hard question."

"What will you do today?"

With a look around for the barmaid, he reached up with a wave for her and turned back to Castro. "Is Ike in town today?"

The man shook his head.

The brown-skinned teenage girl arrived. "What to you need, señor?"

"Some good whiskey."

She put her hand on one jaunty hip and shook her head, bending over enough for him to look down her blouse at her small cleavage. "Whiskey? We got mescal."

"Bring us a bottle of that and two glasses."

"That will cost you four pesos."

"Go get it. I have the money." He shooed her away, not inter-ested in her underdeveloped assets.

Castro laughed after her hip-shaking retreat. "She thinks she's the numero uno *puta* in town."

Slocum warily shook his head. "Not enough meat on her bones for me."

"Yes, I agree. So now what do you do?"

"Like you do, stand back and let them go by. Where is this scarred, fat Gorman?"

The man frowned at him. "Why that one?"

"He's the last leg on the three-legged stool that raped a young virgin in the mountains."

"They did do many bad things. I wondered why you were after him. Good that you already have the other two."

The barmaid brought the bottle and tumblers, set them on the table, and held out her light-colored palm. "Four pesos for the bottle. One for me makes five."

"I'll make it four, thanks." Slocum paid her.

Her dark eyes flashed with anger and she leaned close to inform him, "You don't even know what good ass is, señor."

"Oh, yes I do. I would not pay over ten centavos for a shot at your ass."

"You damn sure won't even get to touch it for that." Nose in the air, she sashayed her hips back to the bar and told the bartender something about "that cheap gringo."

Slocum and Castro both laughed together over her flaunting ways.

He drank lightly and listened to Castro's problems about his wife and latest girlfriend. Both of them were pregnant and due on the same day and he was upset.

"For even more children, I am going to have to breed them back again on the tenth day, like a mare, to get them to stick, and they are twenty miles apart. I'll have to ride a horse hard to do that to both of them."

"You have a real problem," Slocum said. "Will your wife let you touch her?"

"Oh, sure, she loves babies. Mine all have curly hair too."

And it wasn't funny—Castro was serious.

With no sign of Ike and no word on him coming or being in town, Slocum left Castro and went to find some food. Castro was waiting for his pregnant girlfriend to come get him.

A drunk named Horace Mattes stopped Slocum and begged for a quarter. He needed a drink.

"Tell me where Ike is at." Slocum held the silver coin out to show the rumpled, bad-smelling derelict that he had one for him.

"Aw, he's in *Messieco*."

"But where down there?"

"How should I know?" He loudly hiccupped.

Slocum gave him the quarter, shook his head, and went on. No use trying to get anything out of a man that drunk.

Near sundown, he headed back to Tombstone, satisfied that Ike wasn't in Charleston. With King settled in the livery, he walked back to Carla's. When he was upstairs in her apartment at last, the maid Flossie told them that an Indian was downstairs wanting to talk to him.

Since she didn't cater to them, he said he'd go down and see about him. It was the Apache named Benny. He rose from his seat on the swing and nodded. "They tell me you want Gorman."

"He's one of the men who raped Rosa's cousin Nana on their raid."

Stone-faced Benny said, "My wife was raped too. I was gone."

"Nice guys. But Gorman is the only one left."

"*Sí.* He's hiding in the Bronco Mountains below the border. He thinks you fed Valdez to the red ants." Benny looked like he wanted to know whether that was true.

"I should have, but I didn't have the time."

The Apache nodded. "I can go with you in the morning to find him."

"When do we leave?"

"When the moon comes up."

Slocum tried to recall the lunar schedule from the evening before. "What time?"

"Around two o'clock in the morning."

"I'll meet you on the road down there."

"At Spider Creek?"

"That's the place."

Benny shook his hand. "Maybe I can find the ants, huh?"

"I'll bring the sorghum. See you then."

They parted.

Slocum tried to decide if the Apache was serious about putting the outlaw on the red anthill or not. He better bring the syrup along just in case he was. Carla's cook filled a glass jar with sorghum for him.

He and Carla made love in her apartment that evening. At sundown he brought his horse and hitched him behind the whorehouse so he'd be ready for when he must leave to meet Benny. A midnight departure would give him plenty of time to get down there. Carla had a run on customers that evening, so he slept by himself until she came and woke him.

"Time to get up, big man."

"You sure must have had a helluva night's business down there."

"And I don't know why." She turned her palms up and shrugged. "But those girls will all think they slid down a cactus banister tomorrow."

He hugged her, then kissed her mouth. "I may be a day or so, but I want this bastard and we'll get him if he's down there."

She nodded and took him downstairs by the back way, the same way that she would take a married man up to some girl's room. Out of sight and mind. Slocum kissed her again and mounted his horse. He rode down the alley, then headed due south through the desert to meet Benny. Twice he stopped in a brushy draw and waited to be certain no one was on his back trail. He made it to the dry Spider Creek and waited for Benny.

Benny arrived when the moon rose and they rode to Mexico. The Apache knew a back way into the Broncos, a low set of hills, and they soon hobbled their horses in a dry wash to go on foot the rest of the way to the place Gorman was supposed to be. Benny told him to stay under some cottonwoods in a wash and he'd go check on the fat man's whereabouts.

In a short while, Benny came back. "He's here. Snoring like a fat hog in a hammock behind a jacal. I should have cut his throat while I was there."

"I thought you wanted to stake him on an anthill."

Benny shook his head in wary disgust. "He scared my wife so bad she screamed in the night for months after that. She is a good woman. I hated them for doing that to the women of our town."

"It was bad."

"Let's go take him."

Slocum took his rifle and they went with care. Soon they were near the jacal and Benny stopped him. "He is not snoring."

"Does he know we are here?" Slocum asked.

"I don't think so, but maybe his balls told him we were here."

They both chuckled at Benny's joke. Slocum went to the left; Benny took to the right. Closer to the adobe shack, Slocum heard someone out back busting stove wood. It seemed an odd thing to do at night, but it made no difference to Slocum. On soft soles he slipped in through the garden gate.

"Put the axe down," Slocum ordered from the open gate, watching the man's outline for any charge and holding the .45 in his tight fist.

"Who in the fuck are you?"

"Slocum is my name, and I ca—"

With his axe raised over his head and screaming like a crazy man, he charged Slocum. The short man came like a stamped-ing bull, aiming to chop Slocum's head off his shoulders. Slo-cum sidestepped, and a shot from behind him caused everything to vibrate. He turned on his heel and saw Benny standing in the starlight under the gate arch holding a smoking gun.

"Is he dead?" Benny asked when Slocum knelt and felt for his pulse.

Nodding, Slocum rose up. "He's dead."

"We better go. Be daylight soon."

They both ran for their horses and rode off. Benny and Slo-cum parted at Spider Creek. The Apache headed southeast to his place in the mountains, and Slocum went back to Carla, arriving in the early afternoon. With his horse stabled, he came back and took a bath, and she fed him some beef with brown beans. Then they had a session in bed and he slept till seven that night.

News of the outlaw Gorman's death took twenty-four hours to get to Tombstone. Marshal White sent Slocum a note that read:

The outlaw called Gorman was shot by parties unknown yesterday morning in the Broncos. I knew you were inter-ested. Marshal White.

He read the contents out loud to Carla in bed. When he fin-ished, she reached over and began to jack him off. He looked down at her skilled hand pounding his meat and smiled. Then he moved closer and she did the same until he covered her. In no time she plugged him into her vagina and they went to rocking the bed. Her fine pear-shaped breasts jiggled on her chest under him as he pounded her ass, and the smile she wore was as wide as Texas.

Someone knocked softly on her door.

"Not now, gawdamnit!" she shouted, and the knocking stopped. Her eyes were clouded with anger and her breath rasped deep in her throat as she tried to get back in the rhythm with him. Then he came hard inside her. She sucked in her breath, then followed his course, and her hot gush of cum ran out over his balls as he fired inside her again.

When she was able to stand, she put on a robe and muttered, "Oh, damn. I wonder what they wanted." She went to the second-story banister and shouted at the parlor room, "Who did you need?"

She came back in the room. "It was for you. His name's O'Riley."

Slocum began to dress. "Sorry. That would be my fault. I wonder if the Clantons stole another of his horses."

She brushed her hair with hard strokes, seated at the vanity. "I have no idea."

"I'll go see what he wants."

"I sure hope it's important."

"Then we can do it all over again."

"Certainly, after I whip me some black girls' asses so they never do that again. Damn, that makes me so mad."

He buckled on his gun belt and went down to see about O'Riley. Carla still was fried mad, but he tousled her hair as he passed by and kissed her on the cheek. Then he went down to find his man, who was seated in the parlor, moving his stiff new cowboy hat around in a circle in his hands. Obviously not comfortable in the company of the sofa girls in the main room, he jumped up and met Slocum halfway across the room.

"Well, what's wrong? I thought you'd be at the racetracks in Kentucky by now."

"Can we talk outside?"

"Sure." Slocum took him out on the porch. He took a seat on the porch banister and showed him the swing. "Now, what do you need?"

"I want my wife back. Bonnie Jean O'Riley. Can you get her back for me?"

"Where is she?" That was the first time O'Riley had ever told him her name. The man must be serious.

"Preskit is what they call it, huh?"

"Is she still with that horse trainer?"

O'Riley nodded. "I think so. I want her back. I'm no gun-man, and he would shoot me. You he would run from."

"O'Riley, what if she won't come back?"

"Tell her I'll fuck her three times a day if she wants me to. Anything. I can't live without her any longer."

"I want to be paid regardless. There may not be any chance to get her to come back to you. So you will owe me three hundred dollars whether you win or lose."

"You can convince her better than I ever could. All right, I will pay you the money. When can you go and try to get her back to me?"

"In two days."

O'Riley drew out his wallet and counted out the money into Slocum's hand.

When he finished, Slocum again told him he could not guar-antee her return. O'Riley said he understood that Slocum might fail. And he handed him a well-worn photograph of her.

Slocum had gotten herds of cattle back, saved many people's lives, but never talked a woman into going back to a man she'd scorned. Might be a waste of time, but he'd taken the man's money and he never backed down when he said he'd help.

"When I have done all I can or I do get her to consent to come back to you, where will you be?" Slocum asked.

"Hayden's Ferry. I can get up there in one day from Black Canyon City—Arizona Stage Line coach. Wire me there."

"All right. But just so you know, I think you've sent me on a fool's mission."

Head downcast, O'Riley agreed with a slow nod. "Maybe, but I really want her back."

"We'll see."

They parted and Slocum went back upstairs, laughing as he knocked lightly on Carla's door. She shook her head opening it. "You think that was funny?"

Once inside, he swept her up in his arms and kissed her hard. "Got to be something funny happening. All this long-faced business is not good."

"I agree. Let's get naked and chase each other around the room."

"Last one naked is a monkey's uncle."

"Yes." And they were off to see who was going to win.

His eyes were wet with tears of mirth as they finally fell on the bed, still laughing. Crazy woman—she not only was a bed-ful, she had a terrific body. He closed his eyes and shut out the sight of the tin square ceiling tiles. He'd miss her.

21

Two nights later, the stage for Maricopa Wells rattled out of the narrow streets of Tombstone carrying Slocum, with King tied to a lead at the back.

On the dimly lit porch of the stage line, Carla waved good-bye to him. He waved in return, then sat back in the horsehair-stuffed leather bench called a seat. This portion of the trip wouldn't be so bad, but he dreaded the heat in the day ahead. The second leg from Hayden's Ferry to Preskit would be another twenty-four-hour haul north. But high in the pines, he'd find some relief from the desert climate and also, he hoped, Bonnie Jean O'Riley.

The tall saguaro cactus looked like road guards on the slopes and flats of the dry desert. They stopped at the stage station at Picacho Peak first, a place where the Confederates met the California Union Army in the Civil War and the rebs lost. Then the losers went back to El Paso for the rest of the war.

They came up to Maricopa Wells and passed the old house some earlier Indians had built and abandoned—Casa Grande. A peaceful bunch of Indians farmed the irrigated land along the Gila and Salt rivers. They were from the Maricopa, Pima, and Papago tribes, the Salt River Indians. Originally, these people accepted the Catholic Church, supported by the Spanish Crown, and a number of missions were built from Sonora north to Tucson by Father Kino. Other such places were less religiously developed north of there.

Slocum's trip went uneventfully to the ferry that crossed the Salt River and where Old Man Hayden ground barley and corn with a water-powered mill. Slocum arrived there twenty hours after he'd left Tombstone. After a brief rest at a boarding house, he headed back to the stage office to board a different coach. Getting to the stage, he noted another tobacco-chewing driver and he knew he'd have to sit on the off side for the next leg of his journey so as to keep from being soiled from the man's spitting off his perch on top.

A mother and daughter went inside the coach first. Both were attractive women and well dressed. He guessed the mother was hardly past thirty and her daughter eighteen. That made her married and honeymooned at about age twelve. It was a common thing on the frontier for girls to marry young, but they looked more like sisters than mother and daughter.

The mother's name was Emily Dodge and her daughter was Sharon. They conversed friendly-like in voices pitched to carry above the whirl of the wheels, the jingle of the harness, and the plod of the sixteen hooves in the powdery dust. Add the driver's shouts and there was plenty of noise accompanying their ride to the high country.

They, of course, were interested in his background. Married? No. Own a ranch? No.

Have business in Preskit? Yes.

Emily told him he'd love the town and that it was going to be a major city of the West. He didn't care, but agreed with her. Looking at her in the starlight that shone into the coach, he was fascinated by her facial features. Emily was a striking woman. No telling how open she was to dalliance, and Slocum didn't yet know who and where Mr. Dodge was. Her breasts looked inviting under the fine satin dress.

Once on a ride from El Paso to Lordsburg, he'd shared a coach with a woman from Tucson and she'd shared her charms with his dick. With no other passengers in the coach, they spent several hours with him probing her tight vagina and were even bucked off the bench seat to the floor once during the act. They laughed so much about it that when they reached the next stage stop, the driver asked if they'd been drinking.

That night en route to Preskit, the girl asked if he minded if her mother sat with him because she wanted to sleep lying across the back seats. Of course, she'd be in a fetal crouch but said she didn't care; she was tired and wanted to sleep.

Slocum agreed and Emily, trailing the scent of lilacs, thanked him and moved to sit beside him. They absently talked about the price of things and she put her hand on his leg. Her hold was obviously purposeful to him. Her fingers were strong and she pursed her mouth to be kissed. Never a man to deny such a lady's wishes, he kissed her. Then her fingers unbuttoned his fly and undid the buttons on his underwear. They kissed and kissed hard. The woman was quite determined to pull out his pecker and balls, so he slipped his pants down to give her free access to his privates.

Emily went down on her knees and, admiring his dick, winked at him. Her mouth was hot as fire on his erection. When his hard-on reached a stone state, he lifted her up on his lap and, with her straddling his legs, he slipped lower in the seat to make room for his entry. She rose up on her knees, inserted his dick in her wet cunt, and went to bouncing on his lap. A very nice situation for him with her getting hotter and hotter by the minute.

He unbuttoned her blouse, raised her half slip up, and fondled her beautifully shaped breasts. She rode him harder and faster. Then she clutched his shoulders and came with a sharp cry. She wiped her hair back and up from her face and, looking at him with sleepy eyes, shook her head. "Sorry, I am not usually this aggressive."

Sharon sat up on the back bench, no doubt awoken by her mother's outcry. "Have you two been fucking?"

"I wasn't hogging him," Emily said, sounding apologetic as she rearranged her clothing on the swaying coach.

Sharon reached over and squeezed his bare knee. "I guess she got all you had."

"No," Slocum said, and the girl blinked at him in disbelief.

Without a word, she hauled her mother, who was redressing, onto the back seat to get her out of the way. Swaying from side to side, she wadded her dress up until her bare legs showed up high enough for Slocum to see the patch of black pubic hair. Then she straddled his legs and dropped her bare heinie down on his lap. With her hand behind his neck, she drew his face to hers and her hot tongue sought his mouth.

Out of breath at her own discovery, she whispered, "Holy damn, you ain't dead, are you?"

The rising sword from underneath her soon began poking the gates of her vagina. A smile crossed her mouth when his erection reached her ring, and he gave a small grunt as he slipped inside. She sucked her breath in hard. "Jeez, he's sure big enough. Oh, and you just screwed my mother. What was he like the first time?"

"Now, Sharon, talk like a lady. He was simply wonderful."

At that point, she began to bounce on his springboard and she closed her eyes to savor his rock-hard invader. "Oh, this is the best I've ever had. Why don't you have a wife? I'd keep you in chains for my own use."

"You mean you wouldn't even share him with your own mother?"

She shook her head, entirely involved with him opening her blouse and feeling her rock-hard breasts. He really grew fascinated with her skintight tits. She grew even more heated and then, just before she fainted, came all over him. Anxious to get the same pleasures she'd enjoyed, he lifted her off, then put her on her back on the bench seat, folded her like a jackknife, and plugged her pussy with his swollen erection until his gun fired inside her and they both collapsed.

When he got his pants on, she settled on his lap and he raised her up to feast on her exposed breasts. She moaned as he fed on them. Her nipples turned stone hard under his lips and tongue. He at last let her settle in his arms.

With a weary headshake, he exhaled. "Whew, you two ladies are just wonderful."

"You can come out to our ranch," Emily offered.

"What about Mr. Dodge?" he asked.

"He died four years ago," Emily somberly said.

"We'll see. I have some business to handle for a man first."

Her clothes neatly back in place, Sharon snuggled into the seat beside him for the rest of the night's rocking ride up the Black Canyon City route. She said, "You'll like our ranch."

"If you two ladies are there, I know I'd love it."

They both clapped their legs and laughed. "Yes, we are."

Past sundown, the stage wormed its way to downtown Preskit and hauled up before the stage office. Fresh horses and a new driver moved into place. He kissed both women and went down the block to Whiskey Row for a good steak after stabling his horse at the livery. Sharon's words not to forget them rang in his ears. How could he?

After his steak and a beer, he spoke to the waitress. "You know of a woman named Bonnie Jean who came up here a few weeks ago?"

"She from back East? Short?"

"Yes. I have a recent picture." He fished it out and she looked hard at it, turning it to the light.

"Yeah, that's her. She's with some racehorse guy."

He nodded. "You know where they live?"

"Yes, they rented a place west of town, I heard."

He paid her a dollar and she grinned big. "What else do you need?"

"Nothing tonight. Thanks."

"I'll be here," she said and took his money for the meal and tip. Then she did a sashay with her ass as she headed for the ornate wooden bar.

He needed a bath, a clean change of clothes, and some sleep. Then he'd see about looking up Bonnie Jean. At a bathhouse, a Chinaman gave him towels and sent his wooden-shoed wife to get hot water for his bath. She ignored Slocum's nakedness, stood on a chair, and rinsed him with two buckets of water.

"You got big dick." With her finger she pointed to his privates, then covered her mouth with her small hands and laughed hard.

"You want to try it?" he teased her.

"No, no, way too big for me." She shuffled away in her wooden sandals.

He dressed, paid her man, and left the bathhouse. A short time later he was back on Whiskey Row, searching the other joints in the block. He sat on a stool in the Dark Horse Saloon drinking a beer and noticed a woman sitting by herself in a booth, crying. She looked a little like the picture of Bonnie Jean. Was that O'Riley's wife?

Uncertain, he took his beer over to stand beside her booth. "Ma'am, is there anything I can do for you?"

"No," she said, shaking her head full of short curly brown hair. "I did the stupidest thing of my life. I left a good man for another. The one I run off with has now run off on me. Now I ain't got no one."

"Mind if I join you?"

"Not if you don't mind a crybaby." She dabbed at her wet eyes.

"Oh, we all have bad days." He slipped into the booth beside her.

"My folks hear what I did, they'll disown me." Loudly she blew her nose.

"Well, let's figure this out, girl. My name's Slocum."

"Mine's Bonnie Jean O'Riley."

"Where's he at?"

"You mean O'Riley?"

"He was your husband?"

"Yes. I was so dumb to ever leave him. Course, this last guy only wanted my money and my—oh." More sniffling and self-pity spilled out.

When the barmaid came around, he ordered two more beers and settled in. She wasn't far from being drunk, and he felt certain that in her state she'd fuck anyone. She soon hugged his arm possessively and sat with her small butt pressed against him. She had nice cleavage, and from what he could see of her, she wasn't bad-looking. He might as well have some fun with her before he turned her back over to O'Riley.

Later that night he and she drove her horses and buggy out to her ranch. She kept passing out and he'd have to wake her up for more directions on the dark road to her rented place. Under his earlier quizzing, she'd said that her other man had left her a few days before, when she'd told him she was broke.

Holding her in his arms as he packed her into the dark house, he realized how small she was. At the front door, he pulled the latchstring and the thick door creaked open. Some starlight crept in, and he saw the rumpled bedcovers on the bed.

He laid her facedown on the bed to undo the buttons on the back of her dress. He planned to have some fun with her. With the back undone, he turned her over and took off her dress. A store-bought expensive one, that was for sure. Then he took off her shoes, slip, and underwear until she was only wearing a corset.

"Cable? That you?"

"You all right?" he asked her.

"Help me out of this—corset too, baby."

He undid the strings and soon she gave a grunt and he hatched her out of the shell. "Better now?"

"Uh-huh." She nestled her face in the pillow. "You getting in bed? Oh please do."

"I'm coming."

"Yeah, yeah, you said that last night. You never did come to—bed—"

His boots toed off, he undid his gun belt, hung it on a chair. Then he undressed and began running his hands over her flesh.

"Oh, that—feels so good. Oh, yes. . . ."

He fondled her breasts. They were firm but not real big. When he kissed her nipples and ran his fingers through her hair, she snuggled up to him, making *mmm* sounds. Then he moved her short legs apart and ran his hand over her crotch. Her clit was stiff and she raised her legs and spread them apart.

He rose up and pushed the head of his dick inside her vagina, spreading her open. In a sleepy voice she mumbled, "Is that your knee that you're trying to shove in me?"

"No, baby, just me."

"Okay, but go slow. Oh, did you miss me?"

"Sure, I always miss you."

She began to breathe harder. "Oh my God, that feels so good." Then she sighed and started going faster and faster. She got so high she fainted and he finished off on her.

Her screams woke him up. Sunlight was slanting in the open

door, and she looked aghast at the sight of him in her bed. She was shaking and holding the sheet up in front of her nakedness. "Who are you?"

"You know my name. We met last night in Preskit. Don't you remember we were married last night?"

Her hand held to her forehead in shock, she shook her head. "I can't have married you. I'm still married to O'Riley."

He looked in disbelief at her. "You told me you were a widow last night. That's bigamy. Oh my God, you may go to jail for that, and us just married. What'll I do for a wife when you're in prison? Lordy, you might get four years for committing bigamy."

"Was it a nice wedding?" she asked in a quiet voice.

"The honeymoon was too. Wow, you sure are great in bed. I knew you'd be, but it was plumb nice."

"What can we do?"

"Well, I know some folks in the courthouse. Maybe for some money we can get it annulled."

"But I don't have any money—what can I do?"

"First you told me you were a widow, now you say you are still married. What's the story? Where is he?"

She dropped her chin. "It is too long a story to even tell you."

He reached over and pulled her down to his face. "Since we're husband and wife, what can it hurt?"

Then he rose up and kissed her. At first she resisted, then she succumbed to his attention, and they were soon belly to belly. In a few minutes more he was inside her, pumping her ass.

When they finished, she lay sprawled out on her back, exhausted. "Holy cow, you are a real guy. I don't ever recall being that wild or that flushed by doing it."

"When is your husband due back?"

"Oh, I'm not sure. Maybe today."

"Then I better go to town and get our marriage annulled."

She sat up on the bed and hugged a pillow to cover her breasts and belly as if considering the matter. "On second thought, he won't be back for several days."

He rose up and kissed her. "Then we can be married longer, huh?"

She smiled, set the pillow aside, and scooted over with her arms out for him. "A few more days anyway."

He rode off for Preskit on the fifth day, whistling to himself. He had promised her he would hire a detective to find her husband and then he'd convince him to come back to her. She'd kissed him hard before he left her and thanked him for all his help.

He sent a telegram to Hayden's Ferry telling O'Riley that in three days his wife would be waiting for him in Preskit at the stage stop. He was to go with her out to her ranch and take care of her. His return to her was all set.

Next he had the operator make another telegram to deliver to Bonnie Jean in two days.

HE IS COMING ON WEDNESDAY TO PRESKIT BY STAGE
STOP MEET HIM THERE STOP I HAVE EVERYTHING
SETTLED STOP SLOCUM

After all that he tipped the operator two extra dollars. The man promised it would all be handled as he instructed.

His business completed, he paid the board bill on his horse and rode out east to find the Dodge ranch. A cowboy he met on the road told him where to turn off and that he couldn't miss their place. He was still done in from his honeymoon with Bonnie Jean and amused thinking about O'Riley's forthcoming reunion with her.

Getting to the ranch, he saw three white, salt-glazed horses standing hipshot at the hitch rail. Then he heard a scream that came from the house and the sound of someone being slapped. In an instant, he was on the ground, six-gun in his fist.

"Who in the fuck are you?" A man with a five-day beard stood framed in the open window, fighting the wind-whipped lace curtains out of his face. He never got his gun up high enough. Two .45 bullets from Slocum's gun sent him over backward, and more screams came from the house.

Who were they? Obviously they were desperate.

"How many are out there?" someone inside shouted.

"What happened?"

Slocum stood inside the open-sided buggy shed, about thirty-five feet from the front of the house. He reloaded and listened carefully.

"Go out back and go around. I'll keep him pinned down. Go."

The speaker certainly didn't know that Slocum had heard him and was already headed to the back of the shed to greet him when he came around the house.

Through a knothole in the shed's wall, he watched the number two man come creeping along the side of the house looking for him. He only wore a shirt and a cowboy hat. His white, untanned legs looked ghostly. Step by step and constantly looking around, he reached the front corner of the house.

"Drop the gun," Slocum ordered.

The man whirled around too late. Slocum cut him down with two well-aimed bullets. Then he ran to the front of the shed, ready for his partner to emerge.

"Hold your fire. I'm coming out and this girl is my shield. She dies first. You hear me?"

"You hurt one hair on her head and your life ain't worth anything."

"You want her to live, you come out in the open and drop your gun."

"Mister, you ain't getting away. You better give up."

"She won't be pretty dead."

"That you, Slocum?" Emily asked.

"I'm out here, Emily."

"He has Sharon and will probably kill her if you don't do as he says."

"He may anyway." A stream of sweat ran down the side of his face from under his hatband. With him unarmed all three of them would probably be killed. No way he'd let that happen.

"I don't know your name," Slocum called out.

"You don't need it."

"Maybe we can strike a deal?" He needed to make this guy wait longer to act.

"I ain't talking to you. You've got to the count of ten to drop your gun. One—"

"Curly?" Slocum shouted. "I can see you. You go in the

back door. Ralph, you go in the side window. Brandon, you and Harry cover the front door. He's coming out."

"If there is anyone out there armed, she dies. Hear me?"

"Have you ever seen a man's head hit by a .50-caliber Sharps bullet?"

"Shut up and toss that gun down."

"You got the girl. Come on out."

"No tricks."

"No tricks unless you get in Marvin's open gun sights."

"You're bullshitting me. Move," he shouted to her.

They emerged from the front door, him looking around at everything, as upset as a cornered wolf. Sharon's face was as white as ash. He had her by the shirt collar and pushed her ahead, moving toward the horses.

Now would be the time.

"Drop to the ground, Sharon," Slocum shouted.

She obeyed as he tried to shoot at Slocum. The blast from a shotgun sent the man flying to the ground. Emily, packing the pump-action, twelve-gauge goose gun, came toward him on the march, still holding it pointed at the man.

With his gun holstered, Slocum rushed to the sobbing girl's side, crouched down, and hugged her. "It's all over. It's over, darling."

"Oh, Slocum—" She threw her arms around his neck, dropping him on his butt on the ground. Her teardrops, like diamonds, ran freely down her face, reflecting in the noontime sun. "I was so scared he'd kill all of us."

Slocum sat sprawled out on his butt so he could watch the man's dying, his legs twisting his spurs into the dirt. No more of him. "He's not going to bother us again in this life."

Emily set the shotgun down. On her knees, she kissed him. "I never thought you'd get her to do that so fast that I could shoot him."

"We were real lucky."

Sharon snuffed her nose and then rubbed the end with the side of her finger. "Your voice sounded like God to me when you ordered them to put their hands up and to come outside."

"We'll need the sheriff after all this." Emily shook her head. "She's not lying either. You were sent to us from heaven."

"I'll go get him," Slocum offered and started up.

"Sharon there can go get the sheriff," Emily said. "No use in you riding in to town. Then we'd both be out here with these damn dead bastards. Alone."

"Good thinking, Mom."

He rose to his feet. "Take King. We can shorten the stirrups. He's fast."

Sharon laid a hand on his arm. "Don't let her use you all up while I'm gone."

"Sharon, now, you talk like a lady." Emily frowned at her daughter.

"Yes, ma'am."

He smiled. "I'll try not to let her do that to me while you're gone."

Sharon waved her hands over her head. "Aw, hell, you two go have fun. I'll get even with the both of you."

He picked up the heavy shotgun. "We better get some blankets to cover them up with. Those buzzards moving in are looking real hungry."

Emily went for covers. Slocum adjusted the stirrups and boosted Sharon into the saddle. In a flash, she spun King around in a circle on his hind legs and tore out for Preskit.

Emily came back from the house with three old blankets. She handed him one and started to go cover one of the dead bodies.

"You two didn't know these men?" he asked.

"Never saw them before. I think they're all outlaws with a price on their heads."

"Good, we can split the reward."

"No, you can have it. Shoot, we'd be dead right now if you hadn't come by and saved us."

"I'm going to see what I can learn by searching their pockets." He dropped to his knees beside the man he'd shot first through the window and later dragged out off the porch. He hated all the blood on the living room floor. He found a letter.

Dear Casey,

We hope this letter finds you. Your maw died last spring, but we didn't expect you to come back to this country for her funeral. Besides, they got a terrible picture of you in the Harbor Springs Post Office. Our sister Karenia's boy Thadius was stomped to death by a bronc too. He was making a real hand. We'll all be up at Grandpa Perry's ranch for next Christmas. Sheriff Markum may be watching for you if you try to come there. So be careful.

Your sister,
Margie

It was six months old and sweat stained. It was addressed to Casey Jones, obviously not his real last name. Slocum found a bill inside his back pocket for shoeing a horse made out to C. J. Hamblin. He also found three hundred dollars in paper money in the vamp of his boots.

Slocum shoved the money into his front pocket. He covered him up and then went to help Emily.

"I have a letter to a woman," she said, kneeling down in the dust beside the dead leader's bloody body. "It's from Buddy Denton. But it was never mailed. He'd been packing it for a while from the dirt rubbed in the paper."

She gave it to him, then dug money out of the man's boots, vest, and pants pockets, along with a fine gold pocket watch. The wind threatened to blow away the paper money so Slocum gathered it and shoved it in his pants pockets.

The last one they checked, they figured out his name was Larson Moppings from letters on his body. He only had some loose bills in his pockets and some Mexican coins. With the outlaws covered, Slocum and Emily unsaddled the horses and found all the saddlebags filled with lots of gold coinage.

"What should we do about this?" Emily asked.

"I'd say finders keepers. You have a trunk that we can store this in until we decide what to do with it?"

"Good idea. What about the saddles and horses?" she asked.

"Bounty men usually get them along with the guns and any jewelry."

With care, he covered the bodies up, and she went inside to clean out a trunk in the house to store the gold. He packed the leather bags and grunted carrying each one inside the house. There were plenty of gold coins. The folks they stole it all from were no doubt buried by this time. He wondered if anyone even knew the owners' names.

What a mess. He had come here to rest and relax a few days with the two women, and he'd walked into this. He shook his head in dismay. There would be more folks hanging around the ranch after this than he wanted to meet, greet, and talk to. But that couldn't be helped. They needed to get it over with and settled.

With their horses put up in the corral, he helped her fix some food. There'd be mouths to feed. Potatoes were peeled and set out on the wood range to cook. She brought out canned green beans from her root cellar, and then they made the biscuit dough to bake in her large Dutch ovens—no doubt those were used in range roundup camps.

Sprawled out in a canvas folding chair to drink some fresh-made coffee, Slocum called out to her, "Stop and take a break, Emily. We'll have enough of everything for everyone. I checked on that half a side of beef in your cooler—it's all right and I can slice it when the time comes to cook it."

By "cooler" he meant the wet canvas closet that used evaporative cooling to keep beef from spoiling in the summer. The coffee revived him and, wet-faced from the hard work, she finally joined him.

"I should have gone after the law and let Sharon handle this work." She sighed deep and dropped her chin. "Why did them bastards stop here, I wonder?"

He took off his felt hat and let the wind dry his wet hair. "I have no idea."

"You don't make a bad hand at this getting ready business. Where will you be next May? I could use a hand like you in our part of the roundup deal. We provide the cooking and camps."

"I hope miles away from here."

"That ain't nice."

The sheriff and a posse of men pulled up, along with two wagons pulled by some stout horses as well as a doctor's buggy powered by a sweet-looking chestnut Morgan mare. The doc went around and checked each corpse. Some of the men with the sheriff went and looked at the outlaws' horses, hoping to recognize a stolen one. A small clerk wearing glasses took shorthand notes that the sheriff reeled off—records of how the bodies were situated after the shooting took place.

The sheriff accepted Emily's word on most things.

A short, silver-headed rancher asked Slocum what his part in this deal was.

"I guess I was invited over for some apple pie and ended up being a roundup cook. Emily said you all needed to be fed." He nodded at her where she stood motioning for him to start slicing and cooking the beef.

"Hmm." The man snuffed through his nose.

Slocum soon was cutting off slices of beef faster than two more men could salt and pepper them. Someone relieved him on the slicing job and he began to spread the red meat out over the iron bar grill.

"They tell me how you can tell if this beef he's cooking belongs to anyone here."

"How's that, Wolf?"

"It will taste real sweet to him 'cause it's his own." They all laughed.

The justice of the peace came over and began to quiz Slocum. "Do you know these men?"

"No, sir, I never seen them before a couple of hours ago."

Slocum was busy turning meat with a long-handled fork, and the mesquite-oak smoke made his eyes water. He moved the meat in a circular motion around the low grate to be sure none got scorched.

"Tell you what, your honor, when I get this meat cooked I'll talk to you all night about those worthless no-accounts."

The man nodded and went off.

"How is the meat cooking?" Emily asked.

"Be done enough for most in a short while. How is the investigation going?"

"The sheriff is content. He has to cross-check some things on those guys, but he's sure he has wanted posters for them."

"Good. Send someone with a tray to pack this meat over to the main table and we'll start feeding them, if you're ready," he said, looking up at her.

"I'll send someone. This looks great." She smiled and went back to the food table.

The aroma of the meat cooking was well up his nose. He straightened his stiff back and nodded at all the curious onlookers. "It's coming, guys."

At long last, his job completed, he sat cross-legged on the ground and cut his meat with his jackknife.

Sheriff Henry came over with his plate and squatted on his boot heels. "Those two women were lucky you came along. Those men would have raped and probably killed them. I had no idea that such outlaws were even in the country. Guess they hadn't been here long. You got anything else to add?"

"No, sir."

"Well, thanks anyway. I told Emily I'd collect the bounties for the three of you and let them know what I else I found. Thanks again."

"Sure." Slocum went back to eating.

By sundown the sheriff and all the men were headed back to Preskit. The dead men were wrapped in canvas and loaded into a wagon that lumbered back toward town. The justice of the peace never did come back over to question Slocum, which was fine with him.

He and the two women sat on the front porch, worn out from feeding the crew.

"Where are you headed next?" Sharon asked him.

"To bed, I guess."

"How are you going to decide which one of us you sleep with tonight?" She kissed him on the cheek and leaned over to see his expression.

"Damned if I know, ladies." He put his arm around both of them. "But you're welcome to my worn-out butt."

"I say we all sleep in the big bed together," Emily said, then she laughed. "Be like three mink on a riverbank in Missouri. We'll be hopping around all night."

Sharon couldn't stand waiting a minute longer and clutched his cheeks between her palms as she kissed him. Hard, hot, and hungry was how he'd describe her kisses. He closed his eyes and savored her attack.

Six weeks later in Show Low, Arizona Territory, Slocum picked up his general delivery mail at the post office. Inside the flowery, handwritten letter from the Dodge girls was a money order for five hundred dollars—his share of the bounty on the men they'd killed at the Dodge ranch. He smiled. Quite impressive. He'd told them to keep it, but they split it just as they had his time with them. That period in his life and the scent of their lilac perfume was still strong in his memory. He crossed the dry, rutted street, waiting for a farm wagon to go by, and entered the door marked First Arizona Bank.

The lobby was devoid of any customers as he walked to the teller. Slocum placed the check on the counter and nodded to him. The young man spoke up. "Sir, we will need to telegraph the bank that issued this to be certain it is authentic. Lots of forgeries going on these days."

"I fully understand."

"I can issue you a receipt for it."

"That will be fine."

"I also need to tell you there will be a ten dollar fee for our services."

"No problem. When can I collect the money?"

"Is three P.M. too late?"

"I'll be back then. Thank you."

"Please sign it, sir."

Slocum used the straight pen dipped in the inkwell. Then he blew on the paper to dry the ink before sliding the money order under the grill.

"Thanks," he said and rode back to his camp. When he came off the hill to the small cabin and farmstead he'd rented, he could see the thread of smoke from the chimney reaching the sky. The wide meadow was rail fenced. Hemmed in by the pine forest on the hillsides, he could see his horse stock raise their heads from grazing to check out Slocum and his horse. The cooler fall air swept by his face. Wouldn't be many more mornings before the first fall frost silvered the grass.

This would be where they would winter. They'd be sitting pretty with the check plus his share of the gold coinage that he'd split with those two Dodge women—no one even knew they had the gold, let alone where it came from. The winter would be a leisurely one spent up there above the rim country.

Rosa came out the door to greet him. Her smile warmed him. A powerful shame that she and Jim Davis hadn't gotten along. But earlier Slocum had found her again in Diamond City—alone.

With his arms locked around her, he swung her around off her feet.

It would be a good winter for the two of them.

Watch for

SLOCUM AND THE HELLFIRE HAREM

406th novel in the exciting SLOCUM series
from Jove

Coming in December!